LIPSTICK

PROLOGUE

Natasha was tired. Tired of a lot of things. Tired of getting up in the darkness before the dawn's early light. Tired of making the sleepy, squinty-eyed trip on the 6:15 subway into the city. Tired of the existence paychecks she got on Fridays that direct deposited into her bank account. Tired of that damn cheap plastic, ten dollar, made in Japan, digital A.M./F.M alarm clock that sat authoritatively on the nightstand beside her bed.

It jerked her unceremoniously out of her peaceful, dreamy sleep five days a week at five o'clock in the morning. She was tired of feeling directionless. Tired of feeling like she was standing on the sidewalk watching the marching band of life passing her by. She was absolutely tired of answering the phone with the phony, "Thank you for calling Brown, French and Dunn Law Offices" cheeriness that she'd been faking for the past two and a half years.

She'd eventually even gotten tired of the make believe relationship she'd endured for eighteen months of those two and a half years, with Junior Legal Executive Eric French. Yep, he was the partner's too rich, too arrogant son. So when she'd finally had all she could stand of his "God's gift to women" attitude she'd had "the talk" with him.

Fortunately his Daddy cared more about the quality of Natasha's work than he did about his son's dalliances in the employee pool. She retained Daddy's respect and probably his approval for recognizing that her interest in his son was an exercise in poor judgment.

So while sitting at her desk, staring out the window in the middle of a "mind drift", she came to a conclusion. Something had to change. If she continued living her life accepting things the way they were, she'd take the .40 cal. Glock she'd bought two years ago for home protection out of the top drawer of the nightstand and put a bullet in her brain. Well . . . maybe.

For the record, as far as that gun or guns in general were concerned, she'd never really been a big "let's go kill something" person but she wasn't a wuss about owning a gun either. There had been many weekends, as a young teenager, when her patrol cop Dad Daryl, had taken her out into the wilds of Washington, north of Wenatchee, for a little deer and rabbit hunting. He had a real knack for dressing out the game they brought down and taught her everything he knew about guns and wilderness survival.

They spent almost every long weekend that came around in their family owned, coal and wood stove heated cabin up by Palmer Lake. It was just south west of Oroville off U.S. Route 97. He called it "Father / Daughter" time. Not being a "roughing it at a cabin in the winter" kind of Mom, Olivia stayed behind. She would stand in the driveway and waving them off then either go shopping or whatever. Nat' didn't care. She was just happy to be getting out of the city, even if the temperature up at the lake hit the low teens and below.

The anticipation of getting there far outweighed the disappointment she felt when it was time to leave. The end always came too soon. With a sense of resignation, she'd help load their camping gear and supplies into Daryl's light blue, '67 Ford pick-up. It was one of three things he was most proud of. Natasha and her Mom being the other two. With their two .22 caliber rifles, a shared shotgun and Daryl's .357 service revolver stowed in the Camper shell, they'd share each other's radio stations while making the two and a half hour drive back to the 'burbs.

Daryl liked jazz. He'd tune in Chet Baker, Oscar Peterson, John Coltrane. She got to know them all after a while. She preferred Rock. He did a very good job of whistling along with Jazz standards while she'd sing along with the Beatles. The Stones. Janis. He'd smile. She'd be floating on a cloud. Everything was right in their world. It was all rainbows and sunshine.

Natasha didn't have very many heroes in her young life but at sixteen, her Dad was one of them. He was the first one to call her Nat'. A nickname that stuck and made her feel closer to him. Those were the good times they spent together. He didn't treat her like a girl or a daughter. He treated her like a regular person.

Then the day came when their home life took a hundred and eighty degree turn. Olivia woke up one morning, made them a scrambled eggs, bacon and toast breakfast, put together two lunches, saw Daryl off to work and waved Natasha off to school. In their absence she packed a bag. No words of goodbye, no hugs, no tears. Just a one-line sticky note stuck to the refrigerator. "I can't do this anymore."

After that Daryl and Nat's lives were never the same. He got quiet. She wasn't sure who was to blame or if anyone was to blame. She wondered if she was supposed to feel guilty. She also wondered if along with breaking Daryl's heart and spirit, Olivia's leaving had maybe broken some part of his brain as well.

By the time Nat' had finished her senior year in High School two years later, Daryl had developed an up close and personal relationship with quart bottles of Russian vodka. Too many of his nights were spent passed out on the couch. Too many of her nights were spent listening to him snore. She ate alone in her room, keeping the T.V. volume low, so not to wake him.

The trips to the cabin stopped. The camping and fishing gear sat neglected in a corner of the garage. Along with their hats, gloves and rifles. All of it collecting dust and cobwebs. When she mentioned the cabin he would slowly shake his head, "not now Nat, not now."

A new routine began. He went to work. He came home. He drank. He passed out. Repeated the next day and the next day after that. It was a Zombie like existence. She felt broken-hearted and painfully alone. For whatever reason and no matter how you looked at it, she'd somehow lost both parents.

She felt a sense of relief when the time came for her to pack so she could head off to college. She kissed the forehead of a faraway eyed, washed-out looking man, wondering not only where her Father had gone but if he'd ever come back.

In her absence, Daryl let himself completely go. All that time at home alone. He had no one. No one to keep the tenuous emotional fractures in his soul from splitting wide open. No one to take care of his spirit. No one for him to reach out to. She called every weekend and when he didn't answer she left teary messages telling him how much she cared. How much she loved him.

Her years at college came and went. Six years of keeping her nose to the grindstone studying law books. A blur of classes, studies, exams and keeping the boy wolves at bay. She did her best to keep her brain from fogging up emotionally just so she could pass those damn exams. She absolutely didn't want to live with the guilt of wasting Daryl's money or the opportunity.

She worked hard. Studied harder. Snubbed the wolf boys. Got a "she's a bitch", or "she's a tease" reputation. Well screw 'em. She didn't. She did graduate to spite them. Top five in her class. 3.9 G.P.A.

Daryl never made it to the Graduation Ceremony. A gold embossed invitation was sent. Phone calls were made only to have messages left on the answering machine. He'd call back. Talk to the House Mother. "Tell Nat' I'm not feeling well. Some kinda flu or something. Won't be able to make it." Nat knew the real reason. The "sickness" the result of too much "elbow bending".

In her twenty-fourth year, law degree in hand, she came home. Set up life in her old room. The gaunt figure sharing the house, bearing some kind of resemblance to her Father had become barely recognizable. How could this possibly be the same full of life, vibrant man she'd spent all those winter weekends with at the cabin? Unqualified to do any kind of emotional counseling and feeling helpless, she watched him slide further and further down into his own rabbit hole.

He had drifted far beyond her ability to reach. Too far for her to pull him back. He looked lost. Too much time had been spent sloshing around in the bottom of empty Vodka bottles. Her talks to try and salvage what was left of him went nowhere. It was like she was speaking some kind of Alien language. Blank stares. Empty eyes. Once in a while she'd catch the sparkle of a smile in his eyes. A flash for a moment of something recognizable then it was gone.

Her own life was on the move, finishing off the end of her two year internship at Brown, French and Dunn. She was on her way to becoming one of the firm's legal eagles with designs on a career as an Assistant in the City Prosecutor's Office. She could see the name plate on her desk. "Natasha Taylor Assistant District Attorney". Daryl hung in for another year.

She was the one. The one that found him. Three weeks ago now. Six-thirty on a Friday night. The taxi dropped her. Front door unlocked. House still. Quiet. No T.V. "Dad?" She called out. No answer. Queasy stomach. Bottle of Stoly on the kitchen counter. Three quarters gone. No sign or sound of any movement in the rest of the house. She turned the knob on the door leading from the kitchen to the garage. Flicked the light switch. "Dad? You out here?" No answer. There was the truck. Clean. No dirt. Shiny. Something spattered the windshield?

She found him slumped forward, head and chest resting against the steering wheel. His blood-flecked .357 service revolver still in the cold, limp fingers of his right hand. Yellow sticky on the face of the radio. No tears, no hugs, no words of goodbye. One-line: "I can't do this anymore."

She had to deal with it alone. Head bowed, leaning against the driver's side window. Her closed eyes leaking a delicate trail of tears. Zombie stiff legs stilting her back into the kitchen. The phone on the wall cold in her hand while dialing 9-1-1. The circus of emergency vehicles. Probing questions. Sympathetic words. Part of the first responders repertoire. No time to break down now. Maybe some other time.

Going through the necessary details had been tedious. Emotionally crushing. Wrenching her heart and spirit. She had to mature fast. There was no learning curve. The line went straight up ninety degrees.

B.F.D. helped with the Insurance Company paperwork. Helped her track down assets. There was life insurance from the job, along with a separate whole life policy he'd been paying into for twenty-five years. The house was mortgage free a few years back. It was all hers free and clear. Everything was hers.

Olivia had been eliminated as an heir in the new will Daryl had drawn up three weeks after her, no hugs, no tears, no goodbyes silent departure. Her appearance at Daryl's funeral only drove a wider stake into the heart of their relationship. Eye contact was made. 'Liv' tried initiating a smile. Natasha gave her bitter. Cold. Detached. Don't bother.

Then there was the cabin. It had been so long. She wondered what kind of condition it could possibly be in.

If it was even still standing. Almost ten years since she'd seen it. She couldn't go now. Too many memories. She didn't need the emotional grief that would come with seeing it. Was sure she'd never be able to set foot inside it again.

B.F.D. set up the sale through a local Real Estate agent in Oroville. It was sold as is. When all the paperwork was done on everything she had a million and a half in the bank. She had a house that was free and clear. Daryl's $5000.00 a month Police pension was honored by the Wenatchee Police Department. Spotless record with a half dozen Honorable Service Commendations. She wrote a thank you note to the Mayor. Wrote one to the Police Commissioner. For a twenty-seven year old single woman she was financially o.k. She could live well enough off the interest if she had to but with the added Police Pension she wouldn't have to work at all.

She took bereavement leave from B.F.D. Spending her days going to Earl Stroh's gun shop over on Archway Drive where she bought the Glock. Three maybe four times a week she made the ten minute, five mile subway ride. Fired off her anger and frustrations in the basement range under the store. Old plaid shirt, holey-kneed blue jeans and ratty sneakers. She'd run five or six ten round clips through the paper target fifteen yards away. She got better. She got good. Good enough after a few months to keep the pattern in a five inch circle center mass. It was her way of dealing with it. Getting out the frustration she felt inside at being cheated into living a life alone.

She felt relaxed, less stressed after leaving Earl's. Accomplished and in control. She'd done something well. Getting the rest of her life as tight as the pattern on the paper target put a grip of determination in her jaw. It was time. Time to put on her "big girl pants" and deal with it.

She spent the next few weeks going through the house. Cardboard boxes filled with her Dad's unfinished life. The truck had been removed by the Wenatchee Police during the investigation. Evidence processing they said. They returned it four weeks later in pristine condition. Inside and out. The paint polished smooth. The inside sparkled. Another note to the Commissioner. Return note with more condolences. Acknowledging Daryl's lengthy career of service. Pride and professionalism. No mention of his showing up for duty the last year ashen faced with blood-shot eyes.

Then last night sitting at the old oak, family dining room table. Dinner for one. Surrounded by three empty chairs. Her emotional dam gave way. Two bites into her K.F.C. chicken. Deep, gut wrenching sobs overwhelmed her. Half-chewed chicken falling from her wailing mouth. Shoulder shaking. Gut wrenching. Fists clenched, pounding the table. An unrelenting waterfall of tears streamed down her face. Dinner pushed away.

Forehead resting on crossed arms on the table. Tears puddled and pooling on the polished wood. Twenty minutes worth. Nonstop. When she was dry, she felt empty. Hollow. Ab muscles sore from the strain. Headache ripping across her forehead. She'd nuked her emotional hard drive. It was time to start fresh.

Things were going to change. They had to. The determined set of her jaw confirmed it. She couldn't possibly have known there would be a whole new direction that her life would go in. A direction that would leave her well-worn, every day path of "in the box thinking" unrecognizable and out of sight.

ONE

Natasha Taylor entered the 7 – Eleven on Cherry Street across from Triangle Park. Friday morning, five-fifty A.M. It was her morning routine Monday thru Friday since starting her Internship at Brown, French and Dunn. The only difference on this particular Friday was that it was her last day at B.F.D. Her resignation had been turned in to her boss two weeks ago.

No tears, no hugs, no words of goodbye. One-line on Company letterhead to Oliver Brown the Senior Partner. "I can't do this anymore." He'd looked confused but accepted her resignation. Offered alternatives. Offered financial incentives. Offered condolences on the recent tragedy in her life when alternatives and incentives were declined. Wished her well. So on this her last day, she stopped and bought her usual 16 Ounce French Vanilla Decaf along with three Super Lotto Quick Picks. A girl has to have a dream.

As usual at this time of the morning, she was the only customer in the store. Selma who owned the place with her husband William, no last name offered or asked, smiled her usual friendly smile. Nat' thought they both looked Pakistani or East Indian or something. She didn't care. She'd been brought up to have no prejudices. Both her parents had always treated everyone like a person first. She lived that philosophy unless circumstances warranted different.

Natasha appreciated the fact that Selma kept the place open all night. From seven P.M. to seven A.M. she was here by herself. It wasn't something Natasha would ever do for reasons that were soon to become very clear. William would be here to start the day shift at seven and work 'til seven at night. Two twelve hour, mind numbing, glaze-eyed shifts. Nat' showed her gratitude for their friendship with the warmth and genuineness in her returned smile.

"Good morning Miss Natasha." The woman lilted, her deep, brown eyes sparkling with life. Her voice had a melodic cadence that Natasha never tired of.

"Hi Selma." Natasha replied. "A beautiful morning today." She added moving towards the coffee station.

Coffee pots holding four different blends, were soldiered against the far left wall towards the back of the store. She loved the smell of fresh brewed coffee. French Roast, Columbian, French Vanilla and a pot of Morning Blend sat patiently on the warming burners. Sitting on a rack to the left, keeping the coffee pots company, was an assortment of Banana Nut, Blueberry and Chocolate Chip muffins.

They shared rack space with numerous four inch round Chocolate Chip, P-Nut Butter and Oatmeal/Raisin cookies. Natasha turned a blind eye on the cookies and muffins. Dead calories were something she seldom if ever let pass between her lips. She knew habits, both good and bad, were hard to break. She didn't want to start a muffin or cookie Jones that would only sneak "hard to get rid of pounds", on her five-foot seven, one hundred and twenty pound body. There would be no "muffin top" above the waist line of her jeans. Bad enough she shared her coffee with a cigarette.

She'd tried more times than she had fingers and toes to count on to kick the nicotine habit. Gum, patches and will-power. All had failed miserably. "Highly strung" was how the Pediatric Doctor diagnosed her when she was having fidget problems way back in the third grade. He made up his own acronym. Called it N.E.T.S. Nervous Energy Twitch Syndrome. Once you had it you had it for life. Anyway it was the excuse she used. It kept her a pack a week smoker.

"You want your cigarettes with your coffee?" Selma asked while ringing up the coffee on the register.

"Sure, that would be fine." Natasha replied, feeling a pang of guilt in her gut. Bad enough to have the habit, it was made worse by her feeling guilty about it as well. She pulled a ten-dollar bill out of her pocketbook and slid it across the counter. "Don't forget the Lotto ticket." She reminded. Selma took the ten, still smiling, rang up the purchase and handed Natasha her cigarettes, Lotto ticket along with a dollar and a dime in change.

"Selma, do you mind if use the bathroom in the back?" She asked, sticking the pocketbook and cigarettes into her purse. She knew that it wasn't the regular practice of the store to let a string of walk-in customers use the bathroom. Bathrooms were notorious for turning into cesspools of germs and filth when every drug addict and wino that walked in the door had access to them.

Selma chuckled softly while waving Natasha towards the bathroom with her hand. "You go." Selma answered. "For a good customer like you, it's no problem.   I was in there cleaning first thing this morning, so it should be fresh and sparkling for you."

"Thank you." Natasha picked up her pocketbook and coffee and started towards the back of the store.

*　　　　　　*　　　　　　*

Early morning hours. The cunning predator. Albert Tooms. Eyes darting side to side, up and down. Always looking. Watch your sides. Watch your back. Watch the front. Hawk beak nose sniffing the air. In stalking mode. Wolves do it. Lions do it. Scavenging Hyenas do it. Animals hunting in a pack have each other's backs. The single hunter is tactile. Reacts quickly to sudden changes. Changes are dangerous. Can't afford to miss anything. Anything that could spoil the plan. The plan is subject to change in a heartbeat. A living, breathing thing that floats. That flows.

Preyer of and on the weak Albert has a plan of sorts. Not something restricted to or constrained by too much structure. The plan has no edges. No borders or boundaries. It's free-flowing. A cork on water. Bobbing, weaving. Moving this way and that.

The lighted sign over the front door calls to him. The store was open. Hell these stores are always open. They're an armed robbery waiting to happen. Easy in, easy out. A thief's version of quick cash withdrawal machines. Cash in floor safes. Cash in cash register drawers. Twenties, occasional fifties, even more rare hundreds slipped under the drawer insert that held the smaller bills.

Albert looks furtively around. No one. Occasional car. Keeps his head down. Eyes down. Flitting left and right. Don't miss anything. Breathe. Relax. Here's the door. Reach for it. Feel the cold metal. Feel the adrenalin rush.

*   *   *

Life is timing and timing is life. If Natasha had been two or three minutes later along the way in her morning ritual of getting up, going to the bathroom, brushing her teeth, getting dressed, whatever, anything at all, she would've not been pulling the bathroom door closed behind her, when Albert Tooms slithered himself through the front door. Sullen, his heart palpitating, he stood with dampening palms staining the counter in front of Selma.

"Pack of Winston's." He mumbled. Eyes darting left, then right.

Selma could see them darting. She decided she would save her customary warm smile for someone more deserving. Albert didn't mind. Didn't care. Didn't get many, if any smiles anyway. He slunk along through his day silently parting the air, leaving an unrecognizable trail. Grimm had found a permanent home on his face.

He didn't miss Selma's smile. You pretty much have to look a person in the eye to get any kind of personable positive or negative reaction anyway.

Looking people in the eye was not one of Albert's strong points. His eyes were permanently cast down and away. Looking at you from the periphery. If you looked up "shifty-eyed" in the dictionary, Albert's picture would be sitting right there on the page big and bold.

Being back on the street was actually a new development in Albert's life. This morning's trip into Selma's store was his attempt at re-acclimating himself back into society so to speak. He'd spent the previous twelve months out of circulation courtesy "The Washington State Department of Corrections". He'd shaved six months off the original eighteen month sentence by being well behaved. Or as well behaved as a convicted felon could be, considering the circumstances.

His assigned accommodations had been intimate. A ten by ten foot cell shared with George a.k.a. "The Edge" Holmes. "The Edge" got his a.k.a. because of his inclination to carry an eight inch hunting knife tucked in his boot. He used it to convince those with whom he met in his daily travels, that it would be wise on their part to relinquish their belongings to him. Refusing his request, Edge would explain, could be harmful to their health and well-being.

An undercover cop, working drug trafficking down in Little Italy, had been approached by The Edge and the proposition put to him. The undercover however countered The Edge's request. He was able to convince The Edge that though his eight inch hunting knife was formidable and an intimidating persuader, it would be no match against the undercover's fifteen round, .40 caliber, automatic pistol.

The Edge, not being so far down in the evolutionary chain that he didn't quickly notice this disadvantage, shook his head and sadly agreed. Hence his twelve month room and board stay in the "Graybar Hotel."

Besides, twelve months of a bed and three squares was not such a bad deal to an unemployed thug living in seedy motels in the less affluent parts of town. Not to mention the hot showers and satellite T.V. For The Edge it was an upgrade of sorts. A vacation as it were from his normal state of affairs.

It was in the D.O.C. lock-up that Albert and The Edge developed their relationship. The Edge, being four or so inches taller and thirty pounds heavier than Albert's six foot three, two hundred twenty pound frame, assumed a leadership role in their cramped digs.

When it came to committing crimes, he schooled Albert on the advantages of a knife over a gun. Explaining with crystal clarity that knives were easier to conceal, silent and so much easier to acquire. Besides with no paperwork involved, it was harder to trace the weapon back to you. Then there was the much stiffer sentencing that came with perpetrating crimes with a gun.

Albert had thought about it. Had more than enough time to think it through multiple ways, a couple of hundred times. He eventually concluded Edge's concept had merit. So upon last night's six P.M. early release for his attempted armed assault, he followed Edge's advice.

He left the Army Surplus store with a replacement six inch long fishing knife that when tested, shaved a thin roll of fingernail from the top of his left thumbnail. It was that very same knife he now pointed in Selma's direction as she turned back from the cigarette display behind the counter. She held Albert's pack of Winston's out in a hand that as her eyes settled onto Albert's knife, had begun to tremble.

Selma knew she was in trouble. She was alone and unarmed. William brought his .38 Police Special with him when he relieved her at seven but that was about an hour from now. Based on the glowering, mean look of determination this man's face was wearing, she didn't think she could stall him for another minute, let alone sixty of them.

William had told her many times that he didn't think it was safe to have Selma in the store by herself all night but it seems there's no way to tell Selma how to do anything once her mind was made up. She had insisted. William needed a good night's sleep to be sharp for his twelve hour day shift and she would be just fine doing the over-night shift by herself. That had been true for the past ten years. Unfortunately it was not so true now.

"Open the till darlin'." Albert rasped, a low, guttural edge coloring his voice. He slid the hand holding the knife slowly across the counter in Selma's direction. Her lower lip curled back under her top front teeth. She was thinking. How and what could she do to get out of this? Albert provided an answer to their situation.

He would be the first to admit he was not the spring chicken he used to be in his high school days. So Albert surprised even himself when he was able to vault over the two-foot wide, four foot high counter, ending up beside Selma on the business side.

Reaching out with his left hand, he grabbed a handful of the generous locks of dark brown hair that spilled down past Selma's shoulders. With a formidable growl, he repeated his demand.

"I'm not," he snarled, "going to be askin' you again. This is by far the sharpest damn knife you'll ever have held up against your neck." He added in monotone grimness. With his right hand, he quickly moved the cutting edge of the knife up against the side of her neck. "If you want to see the sun going down tonight, I would suggest you punch the keys that opens up that damn cash register. Do it now, then sit your happy ass down on the floor."

He stared into her face through eyelids that had become narrow slits. The eyes behind them dark and evil. Selma didn't doubt he would follow through with his "sun going down" threat.

She felt a slight trickle of warm liquid running discreetly down the side of her neck. Albert had unconsciously increased the pressure on her soft skin. The rapier sharp fishing knife was living up to Albert's words. She had no choice. In her mind it would be the money or her life. Albert moved behind her and nudged her towards the till.

"Do it now!" He barked.

Selma reached her right hand out and depressed keys. The cash drawer slid out with a delicate ring, exposing the bank that she started her day with. It wasn't much. The floor safe in the back office held the night's receipts, almost nine hundred seventy-five dollars if she recalled right. She started every morning at five with a new drawer. Two twenties, two ten's, three five's and a half dozen singles. Albert looked over her shoulder and grimaced.

"That it?" He whined. Releasing her hair with his left hand, he pushed her shoulder down until she was sitting on the floor. "You got a safe?" He asked while grabbing the bills out of their slots in the drawer. "Where's it at?" He demanded looking down into her quickly blinking eyes.

Selma looked up at him and shook her head. "We're a small store." She stated. "We got no safe." She lied. She was visibly trembling now hoping this man would believe her, take the cash he had scooped up and leave.

"Son of a bitch lying whore!" Albert spat at her. "Every damn store like this has a safe and if you don't tell me where it's at and get the damn thing open, you're gonna die right here, right now!" He leaned down towards her and jammed the point of the fishing knife into the skin of her neck. A larger sliver of blood began to run down her neck joining the first one as she squirmed away from the pressure of the knife. "C'mon damn it! Tell me!" Albert barked. "Tell me!"

Selma was feeling faint. She was alone with this madman. It suddenly got very quiet. The hum and buzz from the overhead fluorescent lights and the soft music from the portable radio under the counter began to blend and fade. The sliver of blood tracing the contours of her neck had changed from a trickle to a pencil thick stream. Her eyes glazed, she coughed up a bloody bubble of air. Her body spasmed. Her eyelids fluttered two, three times then closed for one last time.

In his excitement, Albert had underestimated the sharpness of the knife. The M.E. would later note: The knife had "severed a portion of the esophagus, cutting through the right carotid artery and not stopping until the point came in contact with her third cervical vertebrae." Basically she'd drowned in her own blood.

"Damn lying . . ." Albert growled. His eyes darted left and right as he walked out from behind the counter and started for the front door while jamming the disappointing wad of bills into his front pants pocket. Out of the corner of his left eye he spotted movement towards the back of the store. Dropping his head down, chin to chest, he kept moving, hurrying for the front doors.

*   *   *

Natasha finished the paperwork from her trip to the bathroom and dutifully washed her hands. Selma had been right. The bathroom was at least as clean as the one Natasha maintained at home. Selma's however came with a very nice scent of Lavender permeating the air. Reaching out, she pulled a piece from the paper towel dispenser to dry the last bits of water from her hands.

Gripping the doorknob, she pulled the door open then turning back, she grabbed her purse and coffee from the edge of the sink. As she started out the door, she spotted a man of some size coming out from behind the front counter.

Head down, he moved quickly towards the front door. He was holding something in his right hand. It looked sort of like the hunting knife Daryl used when he would show her how to skin rabbits. Her eyes darted taking in the scene. Man, knife, counter, door. Counter, man, knife, door. No Selma. Something was missing from the picture. She couldn't see Selma.

"Excuse me." She said raising her voice to the man's back. He closed in on the front door. Three feet. Her breath quickened. She was moving. Quicker now. Ten feet and closing. Like a wisp of smoke the man slipped quickly out the front door. Coming to the counter. Still no Selma. The man hurriedly turned right without looking back. Natasha froze his lean profile. Her mind's eye recording. Stored it. He rushed past the window, down the sidewalk out of view.

She called out. "Selma?" Where the Hell was Selma?

Natasha turned from the door to approach the counter. She picked up something in the air. A different kind of smell. Her nose wrinkled. It was like the smell that rose up from the pre-packaged, plastic wrapped chicken breasts she opened in the kitchen sink.

Something was wrong. The hair on her arms and neck knew something was wrong and rose to attention. Her quickened heart rate knew. Her tingling skin knew it. She'd gotten her wish. Something in her life had changed but the change probably wasn't going to be good.

Leaning up against the counter the smell got stronger. She looked over and down. Selma sat on the floor her back against the wall. Eyes unblinking, staring straight ahead looking back. Her face looked pale and ghostly. Her neck looked a little bloody. Her chest looked a lot bloody. All in all from the neck down she looked very bloody.

Selma's blood had run down across her chest staining her blouse in a wide swath of red. It continued rivering down her arm and over her hand where it pooled on the floor beside her. She'd heard the term used on the T.V. Crime shows she watched. "Bled out". Selma had indeed bled out.

All these thoughts racing through her brain in a span of three to five seconds. The back of her hand shot up against her gaping mouth. Teeth biting knuckles. Breathe she told herself, breathe. She dug in her purse for her cell phone and frantically pushed 911.

"911." Came the woman's voice. "What is your emergency?"

"There's a dead woman at the 7 Eleven on the corner of Cherry Street by Triangle Park." Natasha moaned.

"How do you know she's dead?" The voice asked.

"She's covered in blood. Unresponsive. I don't think she's breathing."

"Do you know who did this?" The 911 operator asked.

"Uh, yes. Uh, I mean no." Natasha was trying to think. "I mean I saw a man leaving the store. He must be the one who killed her."

"Ma'am, you say there's a man? Is he gone? Are you in any danger?" The questions came rapid fire.

"No. I'm alone. Yes, the man has gone." Natasha replied dully. She unconsciously began stepping back away from the counter. Away from the smell of death. Backing towards the front door. She needed air. Her ears were ringing. Her tongue was feeling thick. She was feeling queasy and a little faint.

"Ma'am," the voice on the phone was saying, "I need you to stay on the line with me. I have a car heading your way. Are you sure you're safe?"

"Yes. Yes. I'm fine." She said while stepping out the front door and filling her lungs with a deep breath of fresh air. She could hear a siren wailing in the distance. Its bawling howl echoing off the multi-paned, glass windowed buildings. Reflecting off the black pavement and hard cement sidewalks. It was getting closer and louder. She turned to face the street. Walked. The edge of the sidewalk looked good. Feet in the gutter. Sit down before you . . . .

Protesting tires squealing five feet in front of her, the black and whites came sliding to a stop. The siren growling down. The killed engine tick, tick, tick, ticking, trying to catch its breath. The thick acrid smell of abused, over-heated brakes filled her nose. It had been a hard run. "The police are here." She said into the phone. "I'm hanging up now. I need a drink and a cigarette."

TWO

She watched as two cops hurried from the patrol cars. She wondered how many times Daryl had done the same thing. One of them, a puffy faced, beefy looking guy was likely very good friends with at least one local do-nut shop owner. He hurried his gelatinous mass up next to her as best as he could. His partner, gun drawn, slowly entered the store through the front door. Do-nut cop's left hand reached into the left shirt pocket of his uniform removing a small notepad and a click-top ballpoint pen.

"You the one that called?" He asked looking down where she was sitting. Her cigarette was barely half gone. She flicked it into the gutter to join the rest of discarded humanity. They'd shown up pretty fast.

"Ya." Natasha replied solemnly. Her eyes fixed, staring across the street at some not to be remembered Dry Cleaners. Time slipped by. "Yes, I'm o.k." She finally said. "In case you were going to ask."

The pen point poised over the page of the flipped open notepad. "You got a name sweetheart." He asked raising his eyebrows. He smiled. Leery. The same look half way drunk customers do at strip clubs when the dancer removes her top and starts shaking her wares.

Natasha looked up. Caught him. She saw the last half of it. He did his best to cast it aside. It pissed her off. Standing, she rose from the gutter. Stepped up onto the edge of the sidewalk. About a foot from his flabby chest. Lit a fresh smoke and spoke.

"Listen fat boy," she began with lips thin and tight. "I'm gonna give you credit, though I don't know why. I'm gonna assume your brain is a tad sharper than your body. So I'm only gonna say this one time." Her eyes bore into him. A rattlesnake staring into the petrified face of a cornered field mouse. "My name is not "*sweetheart*." It's Natasha Taylor. Got it? Write it down. Remember, this is one time and one time only. My Dad was a cop so I know how this shit works."

She took a hit from the cigarette, blew it out of the corner of her mouth and continued. "My address is 7513 West Danvers Dr. It's a house, so there's no apartment number. My phone number is 975.8643. That's all you get." She took a long hit from the smoke and dropped it to the curb. "I'll wait for the Detective and give him or possibly her, the rest of the story. You good with that? I hope so 'cause that's how I'm gonna roll." She gave him a defiant look that he was not really prepared for. Actually he wasn't prepared for any of her at all.

Raising his eyes up from his notes, he took in the look of determination on her face. Waited a second to process his thoughts. "Well Miss, I don't see any point in arguing with you." Taking a step back he flipped the notepad closed. "You wanna play hard-ass with me, I really don't care. You wanna wait until the Detective gets here to give your statement? That works for me too."

He took a step back and gestured towards the black and white hurriedly parked at an angle to the sidewalk. "You can have a seat in the back of the cruiser 'til he gets here." The cruiser's red and blue emergency lights spun slowly reflecting off the polished glass picture windows of the store.

"No thanks." She stated turning away from the cop. "I'll wait outside right over there." She pointed at a spot by the front door. There was a three foot high, eight inch deep cement ledge running along below the window.

"Jesus lady, are you always this hard to deal with?"

Natasha turned to face him while walking kinda sideways towards the window ledge. "Only on my good days. You wouldn't want to be around me on a bad one."

The cop's face had flushed. Either from frustration or the lack of a sugary do-nut fix. It was hard to tell. "Ya, well hang around right there." He said pointing in the direction she was already going in. "The Detective is on the way."

She leaned on the window ledge perching her butt up against and on it. Reached into her purse, pulled out and lit another cigarette. Yep, bad day for smoking. She watched as the street scene began to populate. Two more black and whites and an E.M.T. van. Within five minutes a dirt brown Ford Crown Victoria pulled up. A small, flashing red light perched on the roof over the driver's door. Its spinning red light joined the morning ensemble of multiple flashing red and blue lights.

She watched, taking the driver in, as he eased himself smoothly out the driver's door. A little young, she thought. Thirtyish maybe? Clean-shaven, close cut, light brown/blonde hair. A "Caesar cut" she thought it was called. Reminded her of Steve McQueen. Strong chin, medium lips, nice ears and shoulders, strong looking hands.

His sports-coat and shirt fit his body well. She guessed he went to the gym three days a week. Narrow waist, probably a reasonable resemblance of a four or six-pack under the shirt and she guessed a tight ass. He moved onto the sidewalk. A nothing look glanced her way. Moved towards, then through the front door. She stole a glance as he passed. She was right, he did have a tight ass. She smiled. Couldn't hide the color rising in her cheeks. Held back a chuckle.

Half way through her second cigarette "Blondie" reappeared in the doorway. A longer look her way this time. She caught his eye color. Her conclusion, as best as she could tell from ten feet, was blue-gray. They locked on. Penetrating. Getting a read she supposed. He moved towards her, dark brown sports-coat open, hands in the pockets of his light brown slacks. Casual. Unintimidating.

"Miss Taylor?" He asked conversationally. "Detective Ryan" He began. "It is Miss?" Raised eyebrows, questioning. Partial smile. Nice teeth she thought. Regular visits to the dentist. The good cop in the "good cop/bad cop" equation.

"That would be me." She replied showing a partial smile of her own. "And it is Miss." She added standing now and offering her hand. He was close enough to take it. His were warm and dry. Hers, slightly damp.

She was right about the strength. She could feel his grip. Not too much but enough to let you know he could "out strong you" if needed. He released her, letting his hand fall down to his side. Left knee raised, he rested his foot on the window ledge, left forearm leaning on the upper thigh. The friendly approach.

"I'm sorry about you being involved in all this." He gestured with his head towards the window and the store interior beyond. "Did you know the deceased?" He asked gently.

"I did." She replied, then clarified. "In an "I'm a regular customer" kind of way." She stared into his eyes looking for a read. She was right. They were blue/gray. "I stop in on my way to the subway five days a week. You know coffee and . . . ."

"So you were in the store this morning when the situation occurred?"

She dropped the cigarette. Crushed it with the toe of her right foot. "In a manner of speaking." He gave her quizzical. She'd have to explain. "I was in the back of the store. They have a bathroom. I was in the bathroom."

"So you're in the bathroom doing whatever, did you hear anything?"

"I was in the bathroom going to the bathroom. Peeing if you must know, which is different than whatever." Her partial smile began losing its place on her face, her lips tightening somewhat.

"I'm sorry," he began, "I didn't mean to . . . ."

"No matter, no harm. I'll get over it." She reached into her purse. Bad day for cigarettes confirmed. As she stuck the filter in her mouth, his right arm extended and the thumb flicked the wheel on his lighter. He held the flame up to the end of her cigarette. Cupping her hands around his, she sheltered the flame. A habit smokers have, even in a dead calm. His skin was still warm and dry. She felt something distant, from somewhere inside. A disturbance in "The Force". She liked it.

Releasing the contact, she pulled the lit cigarette from her lips blowing a stream of smoke from the corner of her mouth. Made eye contact. He was a step ahead of her. That penetrating look again. Damn it. Did he read the tremble in "The Force" she felt when their skin touched? Probably. Fuck it. She didn't care. She was past hiding her feelings from everyone else, he might as well be a part of the masses.

"So go on with your story." He said calmly, spoke it easily. The partial smile had grown and there was a bit of sparkle in his eyes. Damn, she'd been right. He'd caught the tremble.

"Like I was saying," she began and wondered why her voice felt a little unsteady. Like a singer with a little vibrato in their delivery. She cleared her throat. Nothing there. "I came out of the bathroom just as this big guy was coming out from behind the counter."

"You get a look?" He butt in.

"Well like I said, I was coming from the back of the store and he had just turned, from behind the counter, moving to the front door. His back was to me." She was feeling incompetent for not getting a good look at his face but what the hell was she supposed to do? She didn't know he'd just stuck Selma. Was she supposed to yell "Freeze? Turn around so I can see your face?

"So by the time I got to the front counter he was out the door, heading down the sidewalk in a hurry."

"So you didn't see his face?" Ryan asked, the disappointment registering on both his face and in his voice. Left foot down off the window ledge, hands back in the pants pockets, body turned to gaze across the street. At the Dry Cleaners?

"I saw his profile for maybe three seconds moving past the window." She said it hopefully.

His eyes fixed across the street. It wasn't much granted but it was more than he had from any of the other witnesses, of which there were none.

He turned back to face her. She saw a glimmer of hope in his eyes. She wasn't sure what it was for. Identifying the suspect or something personal? "Well hang tight for a few more and I'll get you downtown."

"Downtown for what?" She asked defensively, without thinking.

"Mug shots." He replied deadpan. "I'm told your Dad was cop. You must know the routine. I'm gonna need a formal statement, have you look at some pictures, stuff like that."

"Ya right." She acknowledged feeling a little embarrassed. He was right, she knew the routine.

"It's gonna take a couple hours. You need to call anyone, you can do it now or when we get downtown. Up to you." He started turning back to the front door.

"I should call work. It's my last day. I resigned. B.F.D."

"Huh?" He said stopping short and turning back to face her. "B.F.D.?"

"Ya the law firm, Brown, French and Dunn. I work there, or did. I quit." She tossed the smoke into the street. "Today's my last day. I can't do it anymore. The phony political crap. Having to kiss ass and be subservient."

"Oh." His smile blossomed like flower petals in a Spring rain. "Brown, French and Dunn. That B.F.D."

"Is there another?" She asked. His eyes were "fall in" deep.

"Uh, no I uh, guess not." He turned again and stepped back through the front door. He had to finish what cops do when they walk into a murder scene.

THREE

"What do you think you'll do with all this time you're gonna have on your hands?" Ryan asked. Small talk on the way to the station.

He'd informally introduced himself after settling into the driver's seat of the undercover. First name Steve, last name Ryan. Again with the obligatory handshake shared with a sense of genuine warmth. On both their parts.

He drove like he moved. Smooth with little obvious effort. Laser focused eyes surreptitiously darted from windshield, to side mirror, to rear view mirror. To her. Then back through the sequence again. Five minutes in, he moved his glances at her up in the sequence. She noticed. She tried to hold her cheek color down.

"I haven't made up my mind on anything." She said gazing out the passenger side window. "At one time getting a Law Degree and working for the Prosecutor's office seemed like it would be an opportunity for personal growth." Her head turned to the front, watching them overtake slower moving cars on the freeway. "But the Politics got in the way." Her eyes stole a look at his profile. "I failed "brown-nosing" and dropped out of "ass-kissing". It was going to limit my forward progress at B.F.D.". Turning back to the windshield. "So I quit."

He nodded once. "You don't strike me as a quitter." He said while guiding the car down an off-ramp, braking smoothly at the bottom. There was no "back and forward jerk" when the car came to a stop. Just smooth.

"You're right. I'm not." She replied matter-of-factly. "I do know when it's time to cut my losses though." He drove a quarter mile in silence either chewing on her reply, or not. He hung an effortless right into the 4th

Precinct parking lot, gliding the undercover into an empty slot. The shift lever moved into park, the ignition turned off and his door opened all in one fluid motion. She watched him walk to the front of the car, turn and look through the windshield at her. "Chivalry. Not all it's cracked up to be." She mumbled opening her own door and sliding out.

"Follow close." He said starting for a side door on the three story, red brick and glass building. Keypad with a punched in code got the door unlocked and open. As instructed, she followed him in. Close behind. Watched him nod acknowledgments to other officers loitering, lingering or looking up from a desk of disheveled paperwork. Felt their eyes move from him to her. Penetrating.

They walked along a six-foot wide hall with a hard looking wooden bench sitting against the wall. A scruffy looking young kid, maybe eighteen or twenty was handcuffed to a shiny ring bolted to the front of the bench. A two-week or so growth of black hair splotched his face. His dark beady eyes behind narrow slits for eyelids followed our progress as we walked by. Sure he was fixated on my ass as we passed by, I felt violated under his gaze.

About six feet beyond the bench on the left, Ryan opened a windowless door marked with "Interrogation 1" in white letters on a black, 3 X 6, plastic stick-on sign. "Have a seat." He intoned pushing the door wide. "I'll be right back."

The room smelled stale and looked tired. A brown wooden table wearing faded yellow lacquer, peppered with too many cup stains to count sat in the center. A hard backed wooden chair on one side and a hard backed wooden chair on the other, faced each other. My eyes darted away. I let them follow him. Motion still smooth. Brought a smile. I turned back to the room.

I chose the chair facing the open door and sat listening to the sounds of the outer office. Cop banter, two-way radio chatter. "These handcuffs too tight." The kid on the bench. About this time Detective Ryan came back. He stood in the doorway looking over the seating arrangements. "Why don't you sit on this side?" He asked nodding with his head to the chair facing away from the door.

"I'm good here." I replied trying to establish control.

"Well I'm not." He said evenly, eyes flashing. "I need to be able to respond if I hear or see something. I can't see anything with my back to the door." He dropped a thick paged, loose-leaf binder on the table. Let his eyes penetrate my body, my brain, my soul.

A blown rush of air later, I was on my feet walking around to the chair in front of the door. He sat opposite, his eyes relaxed, spun the binder around to face me.

"These are some pictures of the local criminal element that populate our fair city." He began. "Take a look through them and see if any of the faces ring a bell. Relax, take your time, there's no hurry."

I looked down at the blue, hard vinyl cover. The pages inside were about four inches thick. "You want me to go through all of these?" I asked with some incredulity. "This will take the rest of the morning." I fake moaned. I wanted to help but at what cost?

"You drink coffee, tea or soda?" He asked ignoring my protest.

"I drink coffee and smoke cigarettes. The coffee comes with three sugars and cream. I'll provide the cigarettes." I was losing my mood. Fast.

"Be right back with the coffee." He started for the door. Stopped. Turned to face me. "Can't smoke in the building though. Go back down the hall to the door we came in, step outside. The code to get back in is "cops". Relate the letters to numbers and punch it in." He stopped took a breath and let his eyes travel my face looking for a reaction. I gave him sour. "You remember that?" He asked.

I stood. Command presence is something they teach in Law School. If you're going to stand in front of a Judge and jury you better be able to command their attention. I flexed my presence. Saw him waver slightly back on his feet. "Ya I got it." I replied looking him dead in the eye without a flinch. "After all if you can figure it out there can't be too much to it." A slight grin started on his lips. I started around the table. He stepped back out into the hall to let me pass.

"Two sugars and cream." He said as I passed through his personal space.

"Three sugars." I reminded. "You remember that?" I moved before he could answer, starting down the hall to the door. Felt his eyes on my ass. Tough deal being a woman in a male dominated world. Have to do something about that. Wanted to turn and bust him but to what end? What would be the point? The last time she checked herself in the full-length mirror hanging on the outside of the closet door, her ass was o.k. Still tight, still high. Well high enough.

The kid on the bench gave her a raping grin. She wanted to spit in his face but held back. His life was already crap. Crap on top of crap is pointless. She swallowed, pushed the door open and dug in her purse for the smokes and lighter.

FOUR

Three mind numbing hours later she had her finger on the profile picture of Albert Tooms. Ryan had responded to her third call from the Interrogation Room doorway. His eyes locked onto hers from ten yards away. Penetrating. He read the look of satisfaction on her face. Allowed something less than a grimace on the way to a tight smile to settle on his.

"You got something?" He asked walking up into her space. She backed into the room, re-establishing some distance. Daryl had drilled her on space and reaction time. She hadn't forgotten.

"Ya, I think so." She replied walking over to the open binder.

"You think so or you know?" He asked impatiently.

She felt offended. "Hey. I've been in this fetid, thick air room all morning. No one wants out of here more than me. Even the kid on the bench got legs." Her words were hard, chopped. "I wouldn't have called you if I didn't have something." She locked eyes. Held on. Penetrated.

Ryan walked to the binder loomed head and shoulders over the open page. "Where?"

She raised her arm, dropped her index finger on Tooms' profile. "This one." She muttered. "He's the asshole."

Ryan picked the binder up to get a closer look. "You sure?" He asked. "Could you spot him in a line-up? Swear to it in court?"

She nodded.

He stuck a finger in it to hold the page while closing the binder. "Be back." He turned to leave the room.

"Now wait a second here." She began to protest. "I need to move on with my day. I've got a desk to clean out and haul a bunch of crap back to my house."

"Gimmee a minute and I'll ride you." He tossed the words over his shoulder, kept walking. Her eyes followed. It wasn't a minute. It wasn't five. More like ten. She was on her way down the hall, past the bench, heading for the door.

"Miss Taylor!" Came his voice from behind. "Hang on there."

She stopped, turned watched him approach. He stopped just outside her space. She gave him a tedious look.

"I said I'd ride you around. Sorry for the delay. Had to generate a B.O.L.O. on Albert. Where to first?"

His turn for a questioning look.

"B.F.D. on Business Center Parkway. It's on the west side by the Sports Center."

"Ya. I know where it is." He said pinning her to her spot with those damn eyes. "Saw Herbie Hancock there a couple of months ago." He moved in. Too close now. Reached his arm out passed her. Brushed her shoulder with his forearm. Grabbed the doorknob, pushed the door open. "After you."

A small gesture. She filed it. Chivalry. Maybe not so dead. It scored him a point.

Two hours later. He'd been as good as his word. Rode her to B.F.D. then helped carry her stuff out to the car. Rode her back to her house. Helped carry four, one-foot square cardboard boxes of personal office junk into the garage. Hunger. Funny how that happens when you miss breakfast and lunch. Eating may be over-rated but still a necessary function designed to keep the body going. He read her.

"I need to put some fuel in." He said out of nowhere.

She stuck a puzzled look on her face. Sent it his way. "Go for it." She said gesturing towards the four-stacked boxes. "I appreciate your help with all this. Let me know when I'm supposed to testify." She added.

"Maybe by then I'll have my own ride." Locked eyes again. A disturbance in the Force again.

He took a step forward. Six inches from her space. Close enough to smell. Too many of her senses going off at once.

"I meant," he said grinning "fuel for the body. You know eating." He smiled. A real one. She returned it. "There's a place over on Meridian Way. A Mexican place. Five, maybe ten minutes away. My treat." He tried a modified puppy dog look but couldn't pull it off. Too much strength in his face. Command Presence.

"Francisco's." She confirmed. "I know it."

He stretched his left arm out exposing his watch. "Almost five. Let me feed you. You know, a thank you for stepping up the way you did today." Penetrating eye lock again. Damn him.

She brushed a forearm across her forehead. "If you can give me fifteen minutes to kinda clean up some, I'll let you."

"That works." He replied. "I need to call in my "20" let Dispatch know I'm 10 - 7."

She knew the codes. Daryl had turned it into a game. Drilled her once a week.

Ryan turned, started for the brown car. She watched him walk. Deliberate. Confident. It was still tight. Made her smile again.

"The front door's' open." She said after him. He raised his right arm acknowledging. She walked to the side door that led from the garage into the kitchen.

Five-minute shower. Five-minute wardrobe search. Black slacks, light peach blouse, black flats. She stood in front of the one-foot tall jewelry hutch perched on her dresser. Earrings? She shook her head. Too frilly. Ring? Why? Bracelet? She had a watch. Nail polish? Please . .

He looked up when she walked into the living room. His spot on the couch gave him an uncompromised view of the front door. The kitchen was a head swivel away. She stopped five feet in front. Stood. Needing his approval? Damn it.

"Well, well. Kinda not fair." He stated with a half grin. She gave him puzzled. "You get cleaned up and I'm carrying ten hours of funk. Pigpen. You know, Charlie Brown? The cloud following that kid around?"

She smirked, nodded. "I know it. You'll be fine. You're a man, you're supposed to smell." She backed up giving him space to stand. He did.

"Well if you can deal with it, I guess I can." He started for the front door. She led the way. Waited until he was through it, pulled it closed and locked the dead bolt.

FIVE

Francisco's wasn't too busy. Fifteen or so tables scattered around in some kind of pattern that management found appealing. Five of the tables were occupied supporting patrons. She remembered the white wine was palatable. She liked Chablis. He had a Rum and coke. The Chicken enchiladas filled the hole. Smelled better than they were. He finished before her. Some kind of stuffed flat bread she didn't catch the name of. The conversation was disarming and honest.

He had been a cop since he turned twenty-one. Made Detective in four years. Impressive. Intelligent. He had his twenty-eighth birthday two months ago. She'd guessed high. The job had added some time and character to his face. His solve rate was admirable, according to him. Eighty-nine percent average. The others, well they were explained as "never will be solved." Cold cases headed for dust covered filing cabinets somewhere in the bowels of the precinct.

She shot him straight. Abandoned by a flaky Mother. Orphaned by a distraught Father. The look on Ryan's face about a cop who "ate his gun" after years of heavy drinking let her know it ran close to home. He knew a few guys, no details. Didn't finish the thought. He mentioned a car accident. He was twenty. Both parents. Didn't finish that thought either. Like her, no siblings. Like him, independent. Like her, driven. Like her and him both alone. They locked eyes. Dinner was done.

"Ride you home?" He asked standing from the table. He let two five's fall onto the table. A generous tip. Kept his wallet out while walking to the register. She followed close.

"I hadn't planned on walking." She joked with a chuckle giving him an amusing look. He paid the bill.

"No I guess not." He grinned, touched her shoulder. She felt her stomach drop. The Force was in trouble.

The ride back felt like there was electricity bouncing around inside the front seat of the car. She kept her space. Eyes out the window. Street lights basting the walkers. Some holding hands, others not so discreetly holding pint bottles in tightly wrapped brown paper bags.

When they arrived he slipped the undercover smoothly up to the curb in front of the house. He left the engine running. The two-way dash mounted radio was turned low. She couldn't make out the calls but she'd bet her life he could. He turned his head to face her. She felt it and turned herself. They gave each other penetrating.

"Hey, uh, thanks again for all the time and work today." He was getting better with the puppy dog. "I'll keep in touch. You know, with the status. When we pick him up." He was searching for the string. Internal personal thoughts were distracting him. "We'll line a few guys up. See if you can pick him out."

She nodded. "Hey, I'll do what I can." She replied breathing out a long deep breath. "I liked Selma. She was a good person. I feel for William. They were close." She bit her lower lip. "You wanna come in?" There it was. Out in the open. Another long, deep breath. "I can make coffee or . . . " She let it trail off.

He responded by killing the engine, lifting the handle and pushing the driver's door open all in one motion. She opened hers with a sweaty hand. Slid out. Started up the sidewalk on shaky legs. His presence was evident behind her, following as close as a shadow up to the front door. Her hand trembling slightly, the key searching for the hole in the lock.

The Force had gone A.W.O.L. Open the door. Stepped two feet inside. She turned to close it. He was way in her personal space. Eight inches from her face. Hands on her shoulders, he spun her. Used her back to push the door closed. Pushed her hard against it. Pressed his mouth onto hers. She was vibrating. "Oh my God!" She thought.

He disentangled his lips off of hers. "Where?" He asked breathing hard.

She looked over his right shoulder, nodded. Turned his head long enough to spot the hall that he figured led to her bedroom. Sliding a hand under each armpit he picked her up. Glued his mouth back onto hers. Strong-walked her backwards down the hall and through the bedroom door. He laid her back gently. Pulled his shirt apart, popping buttons. Her eyes wide, her heart splurging blood throughout her body.

She worked on the peach blouse. Kept the buttons intact. Why not wear it another time? Flats off. Slacks down. He reached around. Unhooked the bra. It floats to the floor. His pants are down. Prefers boxers to briefs. Random thought. She wondered where it came from. Leave the thong or let him? Too late, he was on it and now scooting her backwards across the bedspread. His lips lowering to her breast.

SIX

Morning came early. Felt a little awkward. Last night was way up close and personal. What to say. How to say it. Do you speak of "it"? What to do wasn't a problem. She wasn't sure how but he was up and moving around by five-thirty. He flushed the toilet. Came to sit on the edge of the bed. Shoes.

"You want coffee or something?" She asked, hoping honestly he'd decline. If she didn't have to, she wasn't going to get up at this ungodly hour anymore.

"Nah. I'm good. I gotta be at the store at six." He stood, swiveled his head side to side. Spotted it and took a step. Sports coat in hand, he stood in the middle of the room, eyes on the bed. Penetrating. "I'll grab something along the way." He turned for the door. "Should I call later?"

She could barely see his face in the curtain filtered pre-dawn shadows. She thought he'd be working on the puppy dog.

"That would be up to you." She said it clean. No attachments.

He was quiet. She was tilted up on her elbow. Her eyes on his outline. Silence gripped the room.

"Right." He started for the bedroom door. "You need anything you call me. I'll write my cell and leave it on the kitchen counter. Right?"

"I'll do that." She replied. He was out into the hall. "Ryan!" She called out after him.

"Ya?" His voice echoed down the hall. At the front door now.

"You shattered the Force." Nothing. No reply. She smiled big. Almost chuckled. She knew he looked confused.

"Times two." He replied. "Times two." She heard the door thump closed.

The engine fired right up. The two-way fired right up. The headlights fired up. The biggest grin he'd worn in a while fired up. He pulled away from the curb tires chirping. He knew she looked confused. He chuckled out loud.

*   *   *

Morning turned into early afternoon. She puttered around with the work boxes in the garage, tossing most of it. Carried a handful of pens and pencils into the kitchen, dropped them in the "drawer of various items". They were in the company of glue tubes, scissors, two screw drivers and odd sized, multi-colored paper clips. You never can tell, was her mantra when it came to hoarding.

By late afternoon she felt a mood coming on. Bastard should've called by now. Whoa! She caught herself. How invested in this guy are you? How invested is he in you? How invested in this guy do you want to get? Three very good questions she could only answer two of. Sixty-six percent had never been a passing grade in any classroom she'd ever been in. She stopped mid-sorting. Screw the rest of the boxes in the garage.

Walked into the kitchen where the coffee pot waited. It was fresh a few hours ago. Didn't matter. There was enough sugar and French Vanilla cream to fix anything. Microwave would heat it up in a minute and a half. She stood. belly up to the counter in front of the kitchen sink. Sipping. Back yard grass needs to be cut. Where was the yard service guy? On strike? She hadn't heard. Hadn't heard from Ryan either. Tilted her head back and belly laughed out loud. A one time bark.

Five o'clock shower had been good. More doctored coffee but couldn't only do a half cup before she tossed it. You can't fix a disaster. This time on the couch in the company of a cigarette, local news on T.V. Blouse, Half Bra and pale blue panties with white Daffodils. Was she twelve or twenty-seven? News update scrolled across the bottom of the screen. Albert Tooms picture centered on the screen. Blonde, poofy-haired talking head with too much hair spray and dark purple eye shadow. Halloween wasn't for another four or five months right? Maybe she was prepping. Getting an early start. She chuckled and listened.

"New developments in the murder of Convenience Store owner Selma Patak." The head's eyes sparkled. "It seems the alleged perpetrator of the senseless murder has been picked up. He was arrested early this morning breaking into a Quick Wash Laundromat on the East side of town. Albert Tooms, a repeat felony offender, is in custody thanks to the quick work of Lead Detective Steve Ryan and patrol cops on the beat." Let's go out to the 4th Precinct and our Action Reporter Debbie Dallas."

Deb's got the fresh look. Shoulder length, wavy, caramel hair sporting blonde highlights. Going for the Farrah Fawcett look. Tan suit. Minimal make-up. Sparkling green eyes. Patiently biding her time, waiting for the next "in studio" anchor gig.

Cut to a camera shot of the front of the 4th Precinct. Zoom in as Detective Steve Ryan comes out the double glass doors. Looks pissy. He'd forgotten to go out the side door.

"There's Detective Ryan now. Detective!" The Debbie hollers out. "Can you give me a statement?" Camera zooms in closer. Ryan looks a little grizzly, needs a shave. The reporter scurries up. Sticks her mic in his face.

"Uh ya." He replies. There's a sudden sparkle in his eyes. "Mares eat oats 'n' does eat oats and little lambs eat ivy. A kid'll eat ivy too wouldn't you?"

"What?" The reporter asks sounding dumbfounded.

"You asked for a statement. I gave you one." He turns towards the parking lot.

"Uh, ya." She stumbles, still confused. "How 'bout a statement regarding the status of alleged murderer Albert Tooms." The reporter now sounding a little pissy. Has an edge in her voice. This question a little harder to dance away from.

"In custody pending further investigation." Ryan replies turning sideways to leave. "We'll know more in a day or two. Goodnight." Ryan turns abruptly, moving with purpose to the parking lot. The reporter trails for a few feet, "what about . . ." then realizes the futility. Stops, turns to the camera and buttons the story.

"There you have it folks." She begins. "Detective Steve Ryan filling us in with all the important details in the murder of convenience store owner Selma Patek and the arrest of suspect Albert Tooms. Back to you in the studio Jim and Beth."

Alright. She told herself. Maybe that's why he didn't call. He was busy chasing down the criminal element. No sooner had the thought come and gone when her cell phone chimed. The ring was the opening measure of Beethoven's fifth. Like her, a little dramatic. She flipped it open. It said "unidentified caller". Putting it to her ear she answered.

"Ya." That's the response unidentified callers got. If they were lucky they got three seconds before she disconnected.

"Hey." Came the male voice, scratchy and tunnel sounding. Damn Service Provider or was it the phone. She could never figure it out. All that damn money generated by Apple, Microsoft, A.T. & T and Verizon and everyone else. They still can't make a phone that sounds better than two tin cans and a piece of wire in a hail storm. Before cell phones there were never any dropped calls or half-heard-sentences. Why couldn't they make a phone that just works? Bastards! She recognized the voice. Disconnected the thought.

"Hey back at'cha." She replied. "Nice rapport with the news reporter." He couldn't see them but her eyes were smiling. "You two known each other long?" She ribbed holding in a chuckle. "I see you have our guy in lock-up. You o.k?" She asked turning serious.

"Ya, ya, ya. No big deal." He stated with smooth assurance. "The black and whites did all the grunt work. Caught him breaking into a laundry. What a dunce! What was he gonna steal? Soap? Fabric softener? A few quarters? Maybe he was gonna shut the water off and ransom the machines to the owner."

She heard the crackle of humor in his voice.

"Well you got the easy part. Booking and fingerprinting. Not really something you'll break a sweat over. Did he resist?" She asked standing and walking to the kitchen.

"No such luck." He said with some genuine disappointment. "Dropped the key picks when the cops lit him up from the car and they found a six inch hunting/fishing knife strapped to his calf. It looked clean but it's in the lab. They'll check it for blood and get back to me. I can only hope he wasn't too careful when it comes to post crime clean up. Maybe we can match the blade to the wound and if all that fails, we have your eye witness testimony." He stopped for a breath and was done. A longer ramble than usual.

She stood at the kitchen sink leaning forward. The back yard view hadn't changed since the last time. "You gonna line him up?" She asked. Her eyes traveled the kitchen counter. Cigarettes. Not seeing them she turned to check the coffee table in front of the couch.

"We'll set that up for sometime tomorrow morning. He lawyered up so we gotta play by the rules. I can call you when a time has been set for the viewing."

She nodded. For herself. "You eat yet?" She asked changing the direction of the conversation. She felt her heart rate turn up a notch. She had a plan. Of sorts.

"Cheeseburger around noon. Nothing since. What time is it anyway?"

Her eyes shot to the clock on the mantle over the fireplace. "Going on six-fifteen. I can throw something in the frying pan." She offered. "You know a couple of chicken breasts, steam some veggies. Maybe some brown rice. Nothing to labor intensive." She noticed her held breath. Damn it. Get a grip Nat. You twelve or twenty-seven?

"Well seeing as I've been in these clothes a couple days, I need to clean up. If for nothing else other than personal hygiene." She heard a car engine start. She assumed it was his undercover. "Let me go home run through the rain locker, change clothes and I'll call you back. Say in ninety?"

"Ya that works." She said walking over to the fridge. "I'll get things started here. Take care and I'll see you in a bit."

"O.K. Kiddo. See you when I see you." He disconnected and she flipped her phone closed. Chicken breasts. Hmmm. Walk to the fridge. Shrink-wrapped two pack in the meat drawer. Fresh from the store three days ago. Should still be good she thought. Alright. Frying pan, olive oil, mushrooms, onions, Teriyaki sauce.

Twenty minutes later the Chicken breasts were skinned, cleaned and ready to go in the olive oil and sauce with the quarter sliced onions and mushrooms. Vegetables were washed and ready for the steamer. No pot boiled vegies would ever cross her lips if she had anything to say about it. Water cooking leaves them wilted, unattractive and bland tasting. Beethoven's fifth. She reached for the cell. Flipped it open. Unidentified caller again. "Ya." She barked.

*   *   *

The bedroom was dark. He noiselessly slid the window up. A sheer curtain fluttered softly in the night air. He could hear her talking. No other voices. Must be on the phone. Good. She'd be distracted. Not listening to him as he climbed quietly into the dark room. He had a plan. He could be patient. Find a place to hide.

*　　　　　*　　　　　*

"He's out." Came Ryan's voice through the speaker against her ear. It was even and distant.

"Out? Huh? Who's out?" Lights were slowly flickering and coming on in her head. Their last conversation. "What do you mean? Don't tell me. You mean Tooms?" She said in disbelief. Her lawyer's brain was churning. "Surely no Judge would grant bail on a repeat felon charged with murder!" She couldn't hide the disbelief.

"It wasn't bail." He replied sounding angry and frustrated now.

"Then what?" She asked. There was tension in her voice now. Rising slowly, she could feel the grip in her gut moving up into her chest, tightening her voice.

"Well shit. He escaped custody." Ryan spit the words out like a bad taste in his mouth.

"What the hell? Escaped how?" She was looking for a place to lean. "You just got him!" Angry frustration. The mushrooms, onions and chicken were half way to done. The water in the pot under the steamer was boiling like the blood being pumped from her pulsing heart.

"He was being transferred to the main jail downtown. Overpowered the cop on the way to the van in the parking lot behind the precinct. Cop got too close. Caught an elbow in the face and lost his gun in the process." He was barking now. Pissed off and dumping his anger on her. She said nothing. Waited for him to get to the end. "That's not the worst of it." He said quietly. "I'm sorry Nat but he has your info."

"Huh? What? What info?" She snapped. Eyes darting around the kitchen. Out the window. Grass still needs cutting. Fuck the grass. Night was past coming. It was here.

"The file we had. The lawyer went over the file with him under Disclosure. They went through it together. The charges, the witnesses, you, your name, address, phone, where you used to work. That was all in there."

"You can't be serious!" She blurted, fingers white knuckling the edge of the counter in disbelief. "Are you guys really that incompetent?" She demanded. Flush-faced she was livid now. Breathing hard and fast. Little beads of sweat coming to her brow and upper lip.

The food kept on cooking. She reached over and turned the burners off. Screw the chicken and the veggies. Phone cocked to her ear. "So I have this straight," she began slowly, "this killer, who you all had in custody, is now roaming his happy ass around the city. And if it's possible, to make this fiasco even worse he now has a cop's .357 gun. Oh and by the way even more worse still, if that's even more possible, he knows who, meaning me, can put the finger on him for Selma's murder. Is that what you're saying Detective Ryan?"

Her hand slapping down on the white tile counter made a loud smacking sound. Her breathing becoming ragged, she waited. Her blood pressure up twenty or so points by now. She could feel it pounding in her ears. "I said, is that what you're saying!" She repeated having not given him a chance to answer the first time.

"I'm afraid so." He said it quietly and calmly. The loud slapping sound made him wince. "We have a perimeter set up." He said defensively. "Ten blocks in every direction. I was in the shower when they called. I'm standing naked on the phone waiting for . . . shit, I don't know." She heard a heavy sigh. Could've been him. Could've been her. "I guess I won't be making it there for dinner." He finally said. "I'll be out. However long it takes. I wanted to give you a heads up in case." He let the words trail. She got the message.

Her heart continued to race. "Right. Thanks for the call. Let me know when or if something happens." Her words cut short. She was a heartbeat from hanging up.

"Oh and Nat."

"Ya." She answered impatiently, her voice strained.

"Keep your doors and windows locked. You got a gun right, get it. Keep it close."

"Ya. Thanks." She flipped the phone closed. Dropped it on the counter. Her eyes turned to the frying pan. Almost cooked chicken looked back at her. Grabbing the handle she tossed the works into the sink. The pot of steaming vegetables were next. Hot water splashed. Vegetables splayed throughout the sink. Intermingled with Olive oil, spices and chicken. Disgust. Anger. How could this have possibly happened? Her gun. In her bedroom. Down the hall from the kitchen.

A slight breeze. Gently kissed her face when she turned from the kitchen starting down the hall leading into the bedroom. She felt it. It didn't compute. Hurried through the bedroom door. One, then two steps into the room. What the hell was that smell? She asked herself. Like sweat and old clothes. Three steps.

A smelly, rough-skinned hand suddenly slapped over her mouth. Big enough to cover half her face. She struggled her best. Squirmed. Can't breathe. Five feet into the room. A couple feet from the bureau. Gun in the top drawer under her bras.

She strained her thigh muscles. Feet digging into the carpet. She tried to power forward. Two more steps closer. Reaching her arm out. Then a forearm wound around her neck. Squeezing. Can't breathe. Still arm outstretched reaching. Sparklers like the fourth of July started going off behind her eyes. Struggle for a step.

The squeezing got tighter. Use those thigh muscles. Push. Push. Her vision starting to blur. Damn it! Damn it! Damn it! Her brain screamed. Can't breathe. Eyes going dark. Loud rushing white noise sound in her ears. One more foot to the drawer. Her face wet with sweat. Her eyes tearing. No air. Then there was no sound. No more breath. No more sparklers. No more anything. Just black.

SEVEN

"Where the hell is she?" Detective Steve Ryan stood in the darkness at the front door of the house on West Danvers Dr. "She can't be that pissed off at me." He muttered jamming his thumb onto the door buzzer again. This time he held it for ten seconds. Long enough for him to hear it ringing inside the house. "Well damn it! If she's gonna be immature about it." He didn't finish the thought. Turning he walked back to the curb and the brown undercover. Sitting behind the wheel he waited. Five minutes. Fifteen minutes. Smoke a cig. Call her phone again. Went to voicemail again.

Five more minutes. No point going back to the door. No lights changed inside. No one came home. No lights changed. No lights. It finally hit him. The whole time he'd been ringing the bell and sitting at the curb, there had been no lights on. No lights.

When he spoke to her before, about dinner, it had been twilight. She would've had some kind of lights on to start cooking their dinner. When he called back to tell her Tooms was loose it was past twilight. Dark in fact. Lights on for sure, if only in the kitchen. If she went out, she'd have left a light on somewhere. It's what people do. No one wants to come home to a dark house. Some people turn on a porch light or a foyer light. Some turn on the porch and bathroom lights. No one goes out and leaves no lights on. Something was off. It just wasn't normal.

He jogged quickly back to the front door. Nothing through the small peeking window in the front door about six feet up. Sidled to the right and peaked through the front picture window. Darkness and shadows was all he could see peeking through mostly closed curtains. He was looking for a sign but saw nothing. He hurried around to the back of the house.

Up onto the back porch. He could look through the window in the back door into the kitchen. Not much of a view but if he leaned way to the right, about to fall off the porch . . . . He saw the mess in the shadows of the kitchen sink. Their dinner. Tossed away like a bad habit. Concerned now. Should he call it in? Welfare check would make it a good entry. It'd at least be legal.

    He jumped off the porch and hurried around what looked like a bedroom window. Jump for the red brick ledge across the bottom of the window frame. Pull up with fingertips. Pays to work out. Gauzy looking curtains. No lights and no view. Drop to the ground. Back around passed the porch to the other side of the house. Whoa! He recognized her bedroom window and it was open. Everything stopped. Reach for the gun.

    Easy now, he told himself. Could be nothing. Quiet footsteps softly on the grass up to the open window only five feet off the ground. Two handed grip on the .40 pointed at the window. Back against the wall just like the training says. Quick poke of the head into the opening. See as much as you can, he remembered. Second look sees what you didn't see with the first look.

    Quick head fake. Looking into a dark room. Nothing but shadows. He thought for a second. Took a breath.

    "Natasha!" He quietly called out. No answer. Nothing. The gauzy curtains floated silently in through the open window and then softly out. Fluttering like an undecided butterfly. He moved his face closer to the opening, a little louder. "Nat! You in there?" No reply. "Crap!" He spit. Frustrated and concerned.

    He left the window and hurried back to the undercover. Jerking the door open, he dropped into the front seat while reaching for the radio. "Dispatch, this is Ryan Sam 47. You copy?"

    "Go Ryan Sam 47."

"I need two units. Send 'em 7513 West Danvers Drive. Welfare check. Code 6 copy? Code 6."

"Copy Sam 47. Two units. Code 6 back-up. 7513 West Danvers. Welfare check. Dispatch to Units 302 and 517. Respond to 7-5-1-3 West Danvers, David, Adam, Nora, Victor, Edward, Robert, Sam, Drive. Officer requesting back-up. Welfare check."

The responding units confirmed receiving the transmission. Standing out of the car, he pulled out his smokes and lit one up. Thinking he could hear engines roaring in the distance he smiled. Give them any excuse and cops love to put their foot down. Surging their units around corners. Car bodies swaying on the shocks, springs and undercarriage.

Hard cornering tires crying out in protest. Hard braking. Brake pads grinding against overheating discs that'd be glowing red by the time they pulled up to the scene. The acrid smell of over-heated, metallic brake pads and the abrupt chirp of rubber as fifteen hundred pounds of metal ceases its forward motion. Engines ticking while trying to catch a breath. They parked at an angle. Bumpers hanging over the sidewalk. Three minutes. Very nice he thought.

He gave both officers a tight-lipped grin. "Thanks guys. Appreciate the hurry." He began while they walked up to the front door. "Here's what we got." He stopped at the front door and turned to face them both.

Officer Mike Reynolds and Officer Grant Wymer. Big men. Both over six-two. Probably weighed two ten, two and a quarter stripped. Barrel chested. Biceps and forearms like sixteen year old boy's thighs. Short sleeve uniform shirts stretched as tight as Ringo's snare drum. Breathing deep and slow, eyes locked, attentive to Ryan's words.

"You know the woman knifed at the convenience store three, four days ago?" They both nodded. Quiet. Listening. Don't speak until you get it all, then be agreeable. "Well this is the home of the female witness. Natasha Taylor. You are also probably aware that the perp we arrested for the murder, escaped custody a few hours ago. Here's where it gets sticky." He gave them both his penetrating look. First Reynolds, then Wymer. They held up to the heat. "I was keeping tabs on the witness and she was gonna make me dinner for time served."

Both Officers eyes sparkled and partial smiles began. Ryan's eyes went severe. The smiles disappeared. "When I got here, there was no answer. I checked the perimeter and found an East side bedroom window open. I got a look in the kitchen window from the back porch and saw there was food dumped in the sink. I'm concerned for the welfare of the witness so we're gonna go in and check. Got it?"

Both men nodded. Another deep breath. Hands instinctively dropped to their holsters. Unsnap. Warm hands on the cold grips.

"How?" Wymer spoke, nodding towards the front door.

"I'm gonna pick it." Ryan replied. "We could kick it but I'm thinking the city isn't gonna wanna buy her a new door if they don't have to." He dug in his pants pocket, pulled out a key ring with long, thin, pieces of metal hanging from it. Some had tiny hooks on the ends, others were flat like a screwdriver. He worked on the lock for thirty seconds, turned the knob and the door swung silently open. "No call outs." He whispered.

Raising his right arm, he gave a quick look to Reynolds, pointed with a finger. Reynolds started quiet heel to toe steps moving to the right of the foyer into the living room. Semi-crouch. Two hands on the weapon. Muzzle pointed straight ahead, chest close, leading the way.

Looking into Wymer's face, he turned and gestured down the hall into the kitchen. Wymer nodded. Same crouch. Same chest close weapon. Ryan walked with him, hand on his low back until they got to where the hall "T'd" off. Bedroom to the left, kitchen straight ahead.

A tap on Wymer's shoulder. Eyes lock. Ryan points a finger at himself, nods down the hall. Wymer nods. Then turns his eyes back front. Ryan would take the turn. Wymer would continue to the kitchen.

Ryan side-steps. Back against the wall. One foot at a time. Bedroom door six feet on the right. Bathroom door directly across. Three more side-steps. Bedroom door close now. He changes sides. Back up against the bedroom door frame. Swing the bedroom door open slowly. Lead with the gun. Furtive glance. No movement. Only shadows. Feel for the light switch. Inside the jam. Flip it up. Bright light floods the room. Some disarray.

He took it in. Backed out. Didn't look good. Touched nothing save the switch. Turned into the bathroom. He could see through the closed sliding glass shower doors. Nothing. Back down the hall, turning into the kitchen. Wymer standing by the sink. He looks from the mess in the sink to Ryan, back to the mess, back to Ryan.

"Kinda looks tossed in a hurry." He remarks quietly.

Ryan walks up looks from Wymer into the sink, back to Wymer.

"Bedroom doesn't look much better."

Reynolds standing in the doorway from the kitchen to the living room. "It's clear in here." He says looking from Ryan to Wymer then back to Ryan.

"She's been grabbed." Ryan says. No emotion. "I'm gonna call it. Get the Crime Scene boys out to bag and tag." Starts for the front door. Stops and turns. "You guys can start taping. Start at the driveway. I want the whole damn thing taped off. Then guard it. No one gets passed. No fingers on anything inside the perimeter." He glanced down at their military style black boots. "Try and keep any shoe prints preserved. Flag 'em, then tape them off." Restarts for the front door. Stops again. Turns. "I know you know how to do it. It's just me being neurotic. Anal. O.C.D. She needs us to be good." Turns again this time strides for the front door. Doesn't stop this time.

EIGHT

It didn't take long. Half hour, forty-five minutes later. The house was fully lit. The garage, front yard, back yard. Lit up like a Hollywood Premier. The cement walkway up to the front door from the sidewalk substituting for the red carpet. Foot print impressions under the bedroom window were pulled. Fingerprints were lifted from the window sill and several locations inside the bedroom, kitchen and living room.

At some point he made it known that his prints would show up. Marissa Jardine, the person in charge of collecting evidence for the Crime Team gave him an "oh really?" look. He responded with a shoulder shrug. He felt her eyes on him when he turned to walk back to his car. Fuck her.

He leaned his butt up against the trunk of his undercover. Dug out a smoke. Thought about Nat. Blew out a rush of smoke into the night air. He had to get her back before he couldn't. He let the thought go. The evidence he'd seen gave him hope. Sloppy criminal. Run the prints, get a name. Get a picture. Get an address from Motor Vehicles. Get the criminal. Save the girl. Wrap it up with a bow. It sounded good. He knew it hardly ever went that way.

   *   *   *

Woozy. Thick tongue. Lips felt loose, sloppy. Dull, achy headache. Blood surging in here ears. Pa-thump. Pa-thump. Vision a little blurry. Eyes locked straight ahead onto a door. Penetrating. Maybe ten feet away. Could'a been twenty. She was in no condition to do the Math. Try to stand. Room starts spinning. Teeter forward. No balance. Falling. This is gonna leave a mark, she thought. Turn your head. Protect your nose. Protect your lips. Cheekbones heal better than broken noses. Missing teeth are a bad look. Loud clattering sound. She went right shoulder first onto the hardwood floor.

What the . . .? Why couldn't she stand? Wiggled her fingers. Felt polished wood under them. She was able to turn her head, look down at her left arm. Duct tape. Wrapped around her wrist, holding her forearm to the arm of a wooden chair. Turned her eyes. The right arm was the same. Her knees felt scraped. Tried for a look at her shins. Then ankles. Realization. She was lying on her right side, wrists and ankles taped to a straight-backed, wooden chair. Could'a been a dining room chair, could'a been a kitchen chair. Pointless thought. No matter.

She looked down. Seemed to remember having a pair of slacks or shorts. She'd had something on at one time. Now there was nothing. Her thighs were bare. No socks. No shoes. She dropped her head down towards her abdomen. . . . Whoa! Wait a sec'. Where's the blouse she'd had on? She felt the hardwood floor on her bare shoulder. She worked her eyes over what she could see of her body.

Still a little blurry. Trying hard to focus. She could see the light blue cups of her 37 C half-bra. She looked further down. Still kinda flat tummy. At least when she was standing up. Size 4/5. Twenty-five inch waist. Maybe that running program she started. Light, pastel blue panties with white daisies. Jesus! She needed to mature up her wardrobe. At least the underwear.

"*FOCUS!*" She barked at herself. Did delirium bring on random pointless thoughts? She was incredibly thirsty. Tongue dry. No saliva. Intensity of the headache increasing. How in the Hell was she gonna get back up off the floor? Better question. How was she gonna get herself out of this? The answer to that question and other random thoughts were suddenly interrupted. She could hear heavy footsteps coming closer.

Making her eyes blink rapidly she tried to get back a little more clarity in her sight. Thank God for adrenalin. The surge was pumping more blood. Sharpening her eyesight, clearing her brain. An odd, sideways looking perspective of the door opening.

Work type shoes came into the room a few feet then stopped. Dirt flecked, stained greenish/brown around the edges. Dark green pants. Wrinkled. Looked familiar. Eyes traveling up. Plaid work-shirt. Sleeves rolled up past the elbows. Thick hairy forearms. Darkly tanned. Top of the shirt open at the neck. More hair. There was a man standing in the doorway. Couldn't quite make out the face. Shadowy from the lack of light in the room.

"What the Hell?" Male voice. Tinged with surprise. He came closer. "Jesus honey you gonna mess up that pretty face doin' that." Bending down he grabbed the side of the chair. Rolled her over onto her knees and face. Quick head turn. Save the nose she thought. She heard him. Breathing heavy. She felt herself lifted off the floor. A sharp jolt. The chair now sitting upright. He had with minimal effort, lifted the chair and Natasha back into an upright position.

He was behind her. Close. She felt his breath blowing on the back of her bare neck. Smelled it. Fetid stale beer breath. His body had the same stale smell. A combination of uncooked meat and old sweat. She traced her tongue over her lips. She felt the split on the bottom one. Damn! She could taste the blood on her tongue. Salty. Metallic. Like the smell at the Convenience Store. Selma's blood all over the front of her blouse, down her arms and pooling on the floor.

She hoped Dental work wasn't going to be involved. She hated needles. She used her tongue to push on the backs of her upper teeth. No movement. That was good. Did the same with the lowers. Good too. She felt relaxed. Or as relaxed as you could feel while being half naked and Duct taped to a wooden chair.

She was focusing better now. Almost clear-eyed. Who in the hell had done this to her? Tooms? Fear began to rise inside her. From what she knew he didn't seem to be the kind of guy that would prolong her captivity. She remembered taking those first few steps into the bedroom. Heading for the top drawer. Heading for her gun. A few more steps and she would've had the drawer open. Had the weapon in hand. Tooms was on the loose. More fear rising. Police incompetence. Stupid-ass Ryan . . . . The thought trailed off.

Footsteps again. Moving from behind around to stop in front of her. Raising her head, she looked the man in the face. Her vision bordering on normal but still a little fuzzy around the edges. She recognized the messy, hanging over his ears hair. That big, thick Roman nose casting a shadow over the dark, black mustache. She knew him. She'd seen him before. It was the damn Lawnmower guy.

"My bad." He muttered. "I didn't want to have to hurt you." He muttered. "I know you know who I am now. You recognize my face." He moved. She worked on following him with her ears. "I don't have a choice. Not now."

She tried not to imagine what those words meant to her situation. "I won't say anything." She started. "If you let me go now, before . . ." She let the words trail off.

"Let you go!" He barked with surprise. "What fun would that be?" He didn't wait for an answer. She didn't offer one. "I see you every time. I watch you walk around the yard. Your denim shorts. Too small maybe eh? A little bit hanging out the bottom." His voice was changing. Lowering in its tone. Getting breathy. Sliding shoes on the hardwood. Closer. The smell of him. Closer again. A hand on her shoulder. Rough skin. Sandpaper. "You walk with your motor running. I see this. All the time. I get a little nervous. I'm confused. I want to reach out." His voice a hoarse whisper. She shudders. Shuts down. The bra straps slip silently off her shoulders.

*   *   *

"Now the best way to get the pelt off, is to start your cut right below the throat, a little above the front legs and run it all the way down to uh, well uh, down to uhmm. . . Just watch." It was her Dad's voice. He was showing her how to skin a rabbit. Daryl dug the point of his eight inch, razor sharp hunting knife into the soft, white, blood splotched fur. As described, he started right below the rabbit's throat and ran the cut down the mid-line to just past where the back legs came out from the body.

They'd been at the cabin. Checking out the four or five traps Daryl set out every winter. She hadn't been too squeamish until the smell hit her. The blood. The stomach. The contents of the intestines. Too much for her to deal with. Light-headed. Her ears began to ring. Louder. Then she was on her back. Looking up at him squatting beside her. Gently rubbing snow on her cheeks. "Hey Nat! Nat! You o.k?" Daryl's voice. Hint of a chuckle. "Natasha. You in there?" Sounded far away. "Natasha!" Farther away still. Echoing off the walls inside her head.

Her eyes blinked rapidly. The smell hit her. Not rabbit smell. The smell of unwashed sweat. Like the inside of a jar of pickles gone bad. Eyes focused, she looked at him. He was half-turned away from her. Doing something at the front of his pants. He turned his head to her. Eye contact. His flitting. Hers penetrating. Digging into him. Like a sharp pointed knife gouging into the rabbit's dead body. His eyes averted. Face unable to hide the guilt. Her breasts. Wet. Unclean. Then she knew.

"You bastard!" She screamed at him. "You fucking asshole!" If she had any spit, any kind of moisture in her mouth at all, it would have attached itself to the words she flung at him. "You better kill me you cowardly fuck!" Her face contorted. The veins and arteries on both sides of her neck bulging rope thick. "When I get out of here I will hunt you down like the piece of crap vermin you are! I will skin you like a fucking rabbit!" Her words hit his back like claps of thunder.

Violated. By scum. The tears started then. Frustrating tears. Not self-pity. Tears of anger. There is a level of dark, scary rage that lives in the deep shadowy corners of our primal brain. It's unpredictable and very, very dangerous. Capable of committing the most heinous of acts.

Slowly turning, he left the room. Closing the door solidly behind him. The sound of a key turning. He was locking her in. Quick left and right turns of her head. Ten by fifteen feet she guessed. Small desk type lamp laying on its side on the floor in the far corner. No bulb. Double bed against the wall by the lamp. Windows boarded up from the outside. Huh? What was up with that?

She was terribly thirsty. Tired now. The headache was stronger. Front and center. Her head dropped. Chin to chest. The smell of him rising into her nose. Why? She asked herself. Why did he do this to me? Now some tears of pity mixed into her rage. The anger no less. I'll kill him. She heard the conviction in her head. I will gut him and cut his heart out. Have to get away. She needed a plan. Tears trickling down her cheeks her eyes closed.

*   *   *

Ryan sat at his desk. He looked through the file and shook his head. "Go figure." He mumbled to no one in particular. Knock me over with a feather the way it all came together. End of a long night stretching into one o'clock in the morning. A "heat seeking missile" rush put on the prints lifted from Natasha's bedroom. The forensics. D.M.V. Record turned a picture and a name. Emilio Santori. Unrecognizable to Ryan. An address in a not so nice part of town. Tooms fingerprints were nowhere inside. Who the hell is Emilio Santori? He pulled up a home number from his data base, grabbed the phone, punched seven digits. Let it ring. He counted six. A groggy "Hello."

"Hey Stan. Steve Ryan."

Lt. Stan Wardlow runs E.E.T. Emergency Entry Team. It's how the Media knows them. Anyway, Captain Frank Jules said there was no way he was going to let me make the bust unless Stan's boys were not only along for the ride but leading the way. I made the call. In the interests of staying employed and providing Stan with some work. Not that he needed it. Seems like he and his crew were out running around two or three times a month. I trained with them a few times. Lotta knowledge picked up. He's a good man. His crew's as tight as a desperate choke-hold.

"It's early. I take it you still have a job?" Stan replied.

"Ya, apparently they can't find anyone else that'll take the abuse."

Couple of beats of silence and Stan started. "Say wasn't it one of your guys that . . ."

"Ya, ya, ya. The transport guy. Screwed up." He answered. "Newbies. Gotta love 'em."

"The story is he's on paid time."

"Ya, Admin' leave with pay. It's like a vacation for screwing up. But he won't follow too close behind the next perp he walks out to the transport van." Chair spin so he can extend his legs. "Hey listen," changing the direction of the conversation, "the reason I called was to have you and your boys hit an address on the east side. A possible kidnap victim inside."

"When you wanna do it?"

"A.s.a.p. would be good. She's been held long enough. I'll shoot you over the address."

Another couple of beats. "Uh, let's see. O.k. I got it. We'll go with the dawn's early light. I'll have the crew there and ready to roll at zero four-thirty. We'll head out and rescue the damsel from the dragon."

"Works for me." Ryan chuckled. "I'll bring do-nuts."

*   *   *

Natasha startled awake. She could hear heavy breathing. It wasn't her. Perverted bastard! She thought. Eyes focused on him. Standing in front of her. Penetrating eyes. Damn it! How long? She had no idea. He'd been feeding her a diet of cheeseburgers and root beer. What was up with that? She couldn't remember the last time she'd ordered root beer. The burgers made her feel heavy and fat.

Untaped for bathroom breaks. Him standing in the open doorway. Wouldn't let her close it. Trying to get passed the discomfort. If she thought she could, she'd have jumped into his face. Fingernails, elbows and knees flying. He'd seen her thinking.

"You don't even want to try anything." He had told her with a stern look. It had been the third or maybe the fourth time in and she was feeling bold. Apparently he could feel it and took a step back from the bathroom door. Got down into a crouched linebackers stance. "It would be a bad idea on your part." He grinned. Eyes riveted. He was bulk. She was a third his weight and strength. There had to be a better way. She had to at least try. Like the rabbits up at the cabin. If only wounded, they would struggle to their last breath. Trying to get back to their hole in the ground.

Maybe when he was taping her back into the chair. She could knee him in the groin. What could happen? He'd said he was going to kill her anyway. Why prolong it? Right after he taped her wrists. When he was looking down. She waited.

"Emilio!" She hollered. He'd been gone for a while. The front door. Closed with a thud. She could smell the food. "God not again." She muttered. The smell was familiar. The key in the lock. The door opens and in he comes carrying a takeout bag. "Hey I need the bathroom." Her eyes. Give him nothing she tells herself.

He walks the bag over to the bed. Drops it. Turns to her. Out comes the knife from inside his left boot. Three steps and he's standing in front. She needs to oxygenate her muscles. Take deep breaths. He always does her wrists last. Right ankle is first. Have to wait! Have to wait. Left ankle next. She can feel the circulation rushing. Down her legs into her feet.

He stands full up. Looks into her eyes. Penetrating. Give him nothing she tells herself. Give him nothing. Knife blade moves to her left wrist. Be calm. Be calm. Left wrist is free. Wiggles her fingers and wrist. Same as the last time. Same as the time before that. She can feel his stare. Hard. Can feel his heat. Intense. Give him nothing. Give him . . . Eyes closed. Right leg jerks! Bridge of the foot poised. Need a direct hit. With force.

Pain! Pain! Pain! Radiating across her shin. Eyes open. Looking at his groin. The point of impact. Blocked. His right forearm. Her shin striking his forearm. Harmless. Bone on bone. Sucking air. Looking up to his face. Big grin looking back. He shakes his head slowly side to side.

"You want to die before or after bathroom?" His breath smothering her face like a killer's pillow. A quick sidestep. Around behind her. He grabs a handful of her hair. "You don't move!" He commands. "I cut your other wrist free. You go bathroom. Then maybe I slice you from ear to ear. Give you a big happy face under your chin."

Her right wrist is free. Circulation into her fingers. He jerks her straight up by the hair. Walking behind. Marches her to the bathroom. Pushes the back of her head. Propelled towards the toilet. Arms and hands out to keep from crashing. Head down. Resignation. She's never liked failing. At anything.

She turned around to face him but refused to look him in the eye. Sitting down, she does her business. Cleans. Stands. Head still down.

"Back to chair!" He orders. He stands back from the door. Gives her passage. She passes. Inches apart. He's breathing heavy. She can hear him. Go ahead. Stick me. Get it over with. She knew Ryan was looking. Could feel his energy. But how long was that going to take? She could feel Lawnmower's eyes on her. Following her into the bedroom. Watching her walk to the chair. Light blue with white daisies. Left. Right. Left. Right.

The tape grips her skin like an unwanted kiss. Unavoidable. The skin long since becoming red and raw from the abuse. Wrists taped to opposite chair arms this time. Not so bad now but not so good in a couple hours. Triceps would start burning. Forearms would begin aching. He crouches off to the side. Learned his lesson. Changes the taped leg configuration. Matching the arms. Left ankle now crossed over the right taped to the right chair leg. No screw-ups this time. Right ankle taped to the left.

She sat with legs crossed. Arms crossed. Shoulder burn from stretched arms was a glimmer in the distance. He's done this before she thinks. Heavy sigh when done. He stands. He towers over her. She doesn't intimidate. Hasn't been in worse situations but has been confronted by more powerful men. Command presence.

"Take a good look asshole!" She snapped. "This will be the last memory you have right before I put a bullet in your brain." She turned her head. Eyes closed. She felt the beginnings of tears starting down her cheeks.

From somewhere inside her head a movie starts playing. Daryl and her sitting around the six foot Maple table eating fresh caught and cooked Rabbit. Daryl had grilled it over the fire pit in front of the cabin. Roasted potatoes and carrots in separate tin foil pouches. They were smiling at how good the taste was. Potatoes with lots of butter. Rabbit brushed with his special sauce while it cooked. That was her job. Basting. A three inch paint brush dipped into a cereal bowl. The sauce sizzling as it dripped onto the hot coals. The movie was interrupted by the sound of a closed door.

Eyes open. The room as it was when she drifted off the last time. Small desk lamp lying on the floor. Light blue bra. Flowered panties. She could feel the Goosebumps. The room was chilly. Arm muscles tightening, left arm stretched over right arm across her chest. Shoulders starting to burn. Crossed knees beginning to ache. Hips getting painful. Breathe, she told herself. Ryan! I need you. I need you now!

* * *

The E.E.T. van pulled up to the address. Ryan's brown undercover close behind. Six man team exits the van. Cinched tight vests on all parties. Weapons charged. Locked and loaded. Ryan slips into his own vest. Four-forty Wednesday morning. .40 Cal on the hip. Stan's boys would go in first. Ryan would wait for the clear.

They grouped around the back of the van. Daylight starting. Light pink and orange streaking a pale blue sky to the east. Linebacker looking dude, Don Wymer, older brother to beat cop Grant. Holds the door breach one-handed like it's a hockey stick. Meaty hand and fingers wrapped around the center handle. He's used it before. The breaching ram is a short battering ram. About fifty pounds, three feet long. You swing it into the lock by the door knob causing the hardware and the wood to explode. One good swing and you're in.

Adrenalin's up. We're on the porch. Wymer gets two good prep swings going for momentum and then lets the breach fly. Jesus Christ! Does its job. Door fractures by the lock and swings wide open.

"Natasha!" I called as soon as I was inside the foyer.

"Ryan?" Distant voice. Muffled. Weak. Plaintive.

Loud shouts of "Clear" coming from different rooms. Six big men scurrying. Half crouched, weapons chest high, pointing forward.

The sound of a door shattering. Back side of the house.

"In here!" A strong male voice shouts. I run towards it. Burst into a room at the back of the house. She's there. Wrists and ankles Duct taped to a wooden, dinner chair. Hair stringy looking. Tired eyes. Frail looking. Light blue bra, panties with white daisies. Shaking.

"Cut her loose!" Someone barks. Stan hurries up to her. Pulls out a wicked looking knife. Cuts the tape like butter. Hands free. Ankles free.

"Where is he?" I shout. Face contorted with anger and empathy.

"Gone." She mumbles.

"What?" Cut and angry.

"He's gone. I don't know where. Don't know when. No time. No windows. Day, night, all the same."

"I need to know. Who is it Nat? Who is Emilio Santori?"

"The asshole Lawnmower guy." She vomits the words out. "The son-of-a-bitch who comes around and cuts the grass. Rakes the leaves. Pulls a weed or two once in a while." Her head shakes from side to side. "Said he's been watching me. The fucking Lawnmower guy."

"Ryan. Let's get out." Stan taking control. Six vested, helmeted, black nylon jump suited bodies lead the way. Pulling a blanket of the bed I wrap it around and scoop her up like she weighs nothing. Which she doesn't anyway. We follow.

The morning air is cool. Fresh. Neighbors stand on lawns and in front doors. Amazing how folks just start appearing out of nowhere. Some kind of internal osmosis communication. Befuddled looks paint their faces. Ya, ya, ya. I slide Natasha in the front seat of the undercover. Door closed. Look for Stan. Find him by the driver's door of the E.E.T. van. Quick steps up to him, right hand extended. He grips it. My left hand grabs his shoulder.

"Thanks Stan." I'm grinning like a kid who just had his first kiss. "Helluva job. Clean. Quick. You ever need anything . . ."

He nods. "Hey man. It's what we do. They keep creating and we keep solving. Job security." He smiles big. Right in my face. Brothers in Arms. Unspoken and deeply felt. I hurry back to the undercover and shoot off to the hospital with my rescued fair maiden.

NINE

Two weeks can change a lot. A few days tied to a chair with little water and nothing but cheeseburgers and root beer takes something out of you. I spent the first few days after coming home from the hospital mostly resting in bed. Steve spent them Mothering. Other than psychological I wasn't too damaged. Wrists and ankles were doctored with some kind of salve and healed well enough.

"Get you something?" He asked that one twenty, thirty times over the first two days. Breakfast catered in bed. Dinner catered on the couch. Back scrubs in the shower that turned into playful "shower games." There were brief phone calls from the Precinct. "Need anything? Gotta run. Be there around six." Shows up between seven and nine. Tough job being a Detective. Hours are crap. Appreciation non-existent. Personally rewarding? If you've got that kind of character.

By the end of the first week Emilio Santori. A.K.A. "the fucking Lawnmower guy", had been picked up by a surveillance team watching his house. No money saved from cutting lawns. Pretty much spent on gas, weed-eater filament and repairs to the noisy, stupid-ass leaf blower. No 401K to cash in.

We all end up in front of the judge. Emilio with a Public Defender. Pleads "Not Guilty". P.D. requests bail based on "the defendant's clean background and record of service to the community". The Jerk-off Judge, up for re-election needs the votes so "bail is granted in the amount of $850,000.00"

P.D. pleads, "financial hardship Your Honor. Request a bail reduction."

Judge looks at Emilio. Judge looks at Ryan. Judge looks at the P.D. Judge looks back at "fucking Lawnmower guy" then finally gets around to passing his eyes over me. Doesn't linger. Says to the D.A. "Any objections on Bail Reduction from the City?"

The City shrugs. Nice. Welcome to the Lifestyles of the not so Rich and Famous. Nice to have you in my corner Mr. Hawthorne. First name Lyle. You are obviously not up for re-election.

"Bail reduction is approved." Court reporter types furiously in her Stenotype machine. "Reduced bail amount to be $500,000.00." He says. Raised eyebrows. Looking for approval from the P. D. The D.A. Eyes pass over me again. Don't stop again. Guilt I'm thinking. "Objections?" No one speaks. Prosecutor clears his throat.

"Request a speedy trial your Honor."

Judge magically produces a calendar from somewhere up on his throne. "When?"

"Two weeks?" The Prosecutor knows something. Get this out of the way so he can move on to more important things. Golfing with the Judge most likely.

Judge turns to the P.D. "Counsel for the Defendant have any objections?"

P.D. Shakes his head. "Not at this time your Honor." There's the threesome for golf.

Judge nods approvingly. "We're set for opening arguments. Monday morning 9:00 A.M. the 17th." Picks up the gavel. The next sound I hear is the exclamation point on my day. "Whack!"

County clerk. "All rise."

Obedient puppets all stand to the sound of shuffling feet. We watch the judge harrumph off the bench. Down two steps, opens a door in the wall. Disappears. That's it. Shows over. Nothing more to see here so move along.

Shuffling feet and muted voices start for the double doors. Out in the hall Ryan confronts Hawthorne. "You know you could've held out for the eight-fifty." Ryan and Lyle are face to face. "Maybe even asked for a million."

Lyle gives perturbed. "What? Eight-fifty, a million or five hundred thousand. He's in lock-up 'til the trial date either way." He takes a step back. Ryan's a space invader. I can speak from experience. Ryan takes a step forward.

"It's the principle Hawthorne." Ryan's eyes are dark. Penetrating. Eyelids narrowed. He gives good penetrating. I can speak from experience there too.

Hawthorne's face is pinking up. "He doesn't have fifty thousand. Hell he doesn't have five. What the hell's the difference Detective? As long as he stays locked up. He's not going anywhere."

Ryan takes a half step closer. They're faces are twelve inches. Detective Steve Ryan . . . Space Invader!

"Oh really?" Tight lips. No hint of relenting. "You know whose name the house is in where Na, Miss Taylor was being held?" He waits a beat. Knows Hawthorne doesn't. "It's in his name!" Moves his hands to his hips. Sports coat splayed out to either side. "You don't think that maybe there's a Bondsman in town wouldn't love to take ownership of it for fifty K?"

Hawthorne has realized the pointlessness of taking another step back. "Space Invader" would just press on. "Detective. It's all the man's got. When he gets out of custody in five, ten, or whatever number of years, he's gonna need cash. A place to stay. Something. I guarantee you he's not going anywhere." The Prosecutor's face has flushed a little more. Gone from pink to red. Matching the rose colored pocket square in his light gray, three-piece suit. "Maybe you're too close to this case Detective. Ever think of that?" His eyes move from Ryan's face to mine. Back to Ryan.

I watch Ryan's right hand slide from its hip perch. Fingers clench into a fist.

Uh Oh. Time to move in quick. Wet blanket in the "ready to throw" position. "Well time will tell. Mr. Hawthorne." I say loudly. Move to Ryan's right. My left elbow accidentally hits the outside of Ryan's right elbow. Nothing severe. Deterrent at its most subtle sending a nerve buzz down his right arm. Fingers on Ryan's right hand splay. Not because they want to. It's a Daryl trick. Showed it to me one night while sitting around the fire pit roasting the day's rabbit catch. "Detective Ryan," I begin, "if you have a moment." I start walking, holding his elbow trying to lead him away. The buildings polished aluminum elevator doors are ten yards ahead.

Head turn over my left shoulder. Hair falls into place over the left side of my face. Bacall would've appreciated and approved. Ryan follows shaking his right arm. Opening and closing his fingers. Trying to get the feeling back into his hand. I face the doors. The call button on the right. Lights up when pushed. Ryan puts a gentleman's grip on my left elbow. I wonder if he knows the trick. He doesn't. Or doesn't use it.

"What the Hell was that?" He asks. He's still extending and contracting his fingers. It takes a few minutes for the nerve to settle down.

"You know what happens when two men get in a pissing contest?" No answer. Gives me his best patient look. Resigned. I don't wait for him. Mostly 'cause I don't care what answer he's going to come up with. "No one wins and they both end up with wet feet. I saved your feet from getting any wetter than they already were."

The polished aluminum elevator doors sweep open. I step in. Turn. Ryan gives me a tight-lipped grin lets me know he gets it. Three others in the box as it drops, lost in their own thoughts. Dings on the ground floor. Amazing how quiet elevator doors open. Close the same way. Three of the five in the box are men. They wait. Myself and the other female exit. "Ready for my close-up Mr. Demille." Two steps. Gentleman's grip on my left elbow leads me to the double glass front doors.

Random thought. Do all Public Buildings have double glass doors?

Turn to Ryan. "I'll buy you a beer if you ride me home."

His eyes drop. "Uh, I can meet you around sixish." Eyes up, he looks over the crowd exiting the Courthouse. Nothing more interesting than me. Back to my face. "There's paperwork on my desk six inches thick. Too much time nursing. Not enough time Detecting."

"Should I catch a cab?" There's a little edge in my voice. Damn it.

"Would you?" He asks ignoring the edge. "Should I pick something up?" He asks. Picking up take-out being a man's second favorite thing to do. With or without women. He's either oblivious to or ignoring my frosty edge.

"Surprise me." I reply and start down the half dozen cement steps to the curb. No point in looking back. There's a cab sitting next to the sidewalk. Opening the back door I give the address, settle back, and close the door in one motion. Smooth in. I learned from the best.

"Something I said?" Ryan mutters to himself looking confused. The cab pulls away from the curb. Ryan heads for the parking lot feeling like he tripped over his own feet while going in for a lay-up. Chalk up one for women's team. The brown undercover waits.

TEN

Sitting at the salesperson's desk, I'm giving the Sales Manager a hard look dead in the eye.

"We both know that car has been sitting on your lot for two months." The Sales Manager shoots a stern look at the salesman. Sales managers hate units that sit around. As much as they hate loose-lipped salespeople. The dealer's investment in the hunks of iron not leaving the lot is dead money. Money spent without a return.

I'd seen the car a few days ago. Done a little homework. I think I have this guy right where I want him. "The Retail Blue Book" I begin, "on that 2016 Monte Carlo convertible is four thousand dollars less than the large, black underlined numbers right below the big, orange "SALE" letters painted across the front windshield." He blinked. I waited. He blinked again. Visibly swallowed.

"Now I'm not here in the middle of the night like some kinda Ninja warrior carrying a crowbar. I'm not here to steal the car from you. I'm also not here as a female getting all flustered in a man's Car Dealer Showroom either. I'm here to buy the friggin' car." More blinking. No protests. Is this guy alive? Another swallow. His Adam's apple is getting a workout.

"Well, I uh, somewhere between that Sale price and what you think you want to pay, there's a deal to be had." He turns to the tan faced Greek looking salesman. "Ain't that right Vinny?"

"Oh you bet Mr. Gerard. That's Gospel. It surely is." I want to shoot Vince. Maybe send him back to whatever port he came to this country from.

I turn to Vince. Young. Eager. "Vince, take a walk would you?" Vince turns to Mr. Gerard. Turns to me. I give penetrating. He gets up from the table.

73

"Uh, anyone want something to drink?" He's saving face. "Coffee? Soda? No?" Up from the round table in the sales cubicle. Tries swagger. Doesn't have it in him. Almost trips over his own feet.

"Now". I turn to lock into Gerard. "Wanna sell the car?" He swallows.

"What's the offer?" He's almost done. Breathing quiet. Breathing deep.

"Show me your cost invoice. A thousand over. You pay Motor Vehicle fees. I pay sales tax. You move the car. Salesman gets paid more than a mini deal." I shut-up. Next one to speak loses. He knows the game. Doesn't say a word. Two minutes. Three minutes. Beads of sweat start to show up on his forehead. I'm cool. I'm dry.

He looks down at the foursquare. Car dealer lingo for an eight and a half by eleven piece of paper, with lines dividing it into four semi-equal sections. Top left is their price. Top right is my price. Bottom left is my payment goal. Bottom right is their payment offer. Bottom two are irrelevant. My secret. I'm paying cash.

The beads of sweat have started to trickle down the sides of his face. Still silent. He shifts in his chair. Uncomfortable. More Adams' apple working. He'd win if there was an Olympic category on apple bobbing. Now he knows I know. He breathes a heavy sigh.

"Alright Miss Taylor. You get the car. A thousand over cost. Give me a minute to pull up the deal on the computer." He stands slowly. A beaten man. I give him a disarming smile. Fluttering eyelashes were never my style.

"Now that wasn't so hard was it?" I open my handbag.

He leaves the cubicle. Walks over to a raised counter. "The tower". More car dealer lingo. Goes behind, sits in front of a computer. Types for a minute. Looks over at me. The printer whirs. Pulls the printout comes back to me. Lays the printout on the table.

"Here's the cost." Pulls out a pen. Underlines it. Writes $11,500.00 below. "Your price. Take it or leave it." Establishing control. I take my checkbook out. Write a check for $10,800.00 I know he's padded the invoice somewhere.

"Here's my check. Take it or leave it." My turn for control. Penetrating eyes.

"For cash? We don't even get the financing" He whines. I don't answer. "You are pushing me over the edge Miss uh, Taylor." He's smiling now. No gold teeth but has the look of a prey animal sizing up a meal. I hold the look.

He chuckles softly. "If you ever want a job, you come see me. I'll put you to work. I think you could sell a lot of cars." Turning, he walks out of the cubicle. "Vincent!" He calls out. Vince magically appears. "Take Miss Taylor to finance. Call for a porter and make the Monte ready for delivery." The chuckle turns into a laugh out loud. Walks away shaking his head. Vince looks puzzled.

"You bet Mr. Gerard. You bet."

Forty minutes and fifteen signatures later. The top is down, the stereo is on and the Monte is whisking me off the lot. Deep burgundy body, black top, Chrome rims, black interior. My buddy Eric at B.F.D. hooked me up with an Insurance company. Tags and registration should show up in the mail in a couple of weeks.

Our big day is coming. Lawnmower guy, the Prosecutor, the P.D., Ryan and I have a court appearance. At least now I'll arrive in style.

ELEVEN

It hadn't taken long. Only four months into our dating and Steve Ryan had vacated his sweat box apartment. Took up residence in the twelve by fifteen foot bedroom across the hall from well, my/our bedroom. A desk, two filing cabinets, a computer with a remote link to the Precinct and he was all in. The room getting renamed to "The Office" made it official. "The Force" was put on a permanent vacation. My resignation from B.F.D. turned me into an office assistant for Detective Steve Ryan. The pay sucked. There wasn't any. I get to drive around in my Monte convertible running errands for you guessed it.

His open cases are a few inches thick, piled high on one corner of the desk. I do what I can to keep them in some kind of prioritized order. I'm getting an eye-opening education on how the Criminal Justice System really works. So many cases are pleaded down. So many guilty slugs released on bail that skip out, never to be heard from again. So many truly bad people released back into the streets on frivolous technicalities. Only to prey on the innocent again.

I have no idea how my guy continues to trudge through all the mountains of red tape and still maintain a sense of accomplishment. All the dotted "i's". All the crossed "t's". Finally getting a bonafide case to court where the pond scum perpetrator is "beyond a shadow of a doubt" guilty, only to be given a slap on the wrist. Then getting to walk after serving a third or a quarter of the original sentence. The victim left with no sense of real justice or even worse dead.

I still make time to shoot up targets at Earl's range. The difference? Having someone to shoot with. Ryan. Someone who knows his way around a gun in a professional way. He is shocked at my accuracy. I'm a six inch pattern center mass good from ten to fifteen yards and twenty on good days when my focus is razor sharp. I breathe the air between the muzzle hole and the target. Become one with it. Don't know where it comes from.

It's now the Friday before the Monday of Emilio Santori. A.K.A. "the fucking Lawnmower guy's" hearing, I'm a little on edge. I don't take any pleasure in seeing him again. Let alone being in the same room. It should be quick. Should be easy.

"Don't tell me that!" Its late Friday four thirty and Ryan's raised voice is echoing out from "the office". "I fucking told you! I told you! I told you! I told you!"

I walk down the hall. The office door is open. Steve's standing. Leaning forward. One hand on the desk. One hand holds the phone to his ear. I stop in the doorway. Waiting for eye contact. It comes. There is fire seething in his eyes. Volcanic and unrepressed. I give him quizzical. I get anger. I give puzzled. I get slammed phone in the cradle.

"You know there is a point at which plastic shatters." I say, trying humor.

His head drops. "He bailed out." He says softly now. Somewhat normal breathing trying to return.

I move into the office. Take the chair in front of the desk. Settle in. Cross my bare legs. Shorts are in this week. Temps in the upper seventies. "Who bailed?" I ask a feeling of dread with the expectant answer. My eyes are unwavering on his face.

"Emilio Santori. It's just like I told Lyle outside the courtroom. Found a bondsman who took the paper on his house." Ryan drops back. Thankfully the chair hasn't moved. His eyes end up back on mine. "I'm so sorry Nat. I am really, truly so sorry."

I give him nothing. I'm blank. I'm processing. I'm going back over all his case files that I've read. Cases where guilty vermin have walked on techs. The ones who, like "the fucking Lawnmower guy", bailed out.

Then skipped out. My eyes leave Ryan. They shift to the tan manila folders stacked up multiple inches high. I have had enough. I'm no longer tired. Something internal is stirring. Not the Force. Not this time. Not that one. A different kind. I'm at a "put up or shut up" stage. Shutting up is quickly tossed.

"Don't sweat it." I say calmly. "There's still a chance." I add standing. "Maybe he'll show up for the trial. It's his house. He's got nothing else." I try giving relaxed. Confident. Ryan gives skeptical. He's been lied to before. It's what the criminal element does best. They obviously can't commit perfect crimes, so they become or try to become perfect liars.

He's penetrating. My eyes drop. Hard to look into the face of someone you care deeply for and bullshit them. I probably wouldn't've believed me either. I shift gears. "You'll catch Tooms. At least we'll watch him go away for life." I walk to the door. Stop. Turn.

I give him burning without faking it. I give him penetrating without wavering. "Maybe putting the fucking Lawnmower guy away looks a little sketchy right now. One out of two is fifty percent." I say, my eyes holding his in a death grip. "It may not be what your usual solve rate is but fifty percent is better than zero." I walk down the hall. I've got a plan. I'll give Tooms to Ryan. They have criminal history. Lawnmower guy is mine. We have personal history. Now where, where, where, can I find the tools of my new trade?

Ryan stood, watching her walk away. She looked different somehow. It wasn't the braless tank top. Wasn't the tight shorts gripping her from behind. They were her usual "walk around the house" fare. This was a different kind of different. Sounded different. Body language looked different. Purposeful.

He wasn't sure what but it was there. He almost called her back. Needed to know what was going on. Took a breath to call her name. It turned into a heavy sigh. He started digging. Pulled the Tooms file. "Albert where are you?" He muttered softly. "Bet your ass I'm gonna find you." His jaw tightened. Lips became a tight, thin line. Eyelids narrowed. Resolve filled him. Right now he'd take fifty percent. Fifty percent of something was better than one hundred percent of nothing. It was, like she said. It was better than zero.

*   *   *

Leaning with his back up against the headboard, Albert Tooms reclined. Eyes distracted by the flickering picture on the 19" color T.V., he was thinking. An old saying came to mind. "Life was what you made it". A frown started to grow. It was obvious he hadn't made much of his.

He was laying low. "On the lamb" if you wanted to "Cagney" it up. He felt sour. He was a High School dropout. Two times in ninth grade. Two times in the tenth grade. That was where he drew the line! He wasn't higher education material. He was action. Always bored. Needing the next adrenalin rush. Classic O.C.D. / A.D.D. Without the diagnose. No meds provided. No meds needed. He'd deal with it, not knowing why he always felt anxious. Always felt intense.

The room was small. Cheap. Twenty bucks a week. Minimally furnished. A bed, a four drawer dresser. A half-size fridge with an over active freezer that was in desperate need of defrosting. So much so that the space between the top and bottom wasn't wide enough to squeeze anything in it. A rust stained sink with hot and cold handles that squeaked when you turned them.

Fourth floor. Number four ten. Right by the elevator. Perfect for those who don't require much sleep. The son-of-a-bitch elevator rattled and clanged. Grinded like ghosts banging chains off the cement walls of a mid-evil castle every time it was called into service.

The toilet was community. Down the hall. Reminded him of High School. Stalls lined up against the wall. Doors with broken locks. Toilets with flush handles he couldn't bring himself to touch. Flushed them with the toe of his shoe.

Did the "hover/squat" over the bowl to poop. Couldn't afford to catch some kind of crawling or jumping bacteria that required a Doctor or even more expensive, a prescription. A less resilient human would've caved. He wasn't caving. He accepted his lot, endeavoring to make the best of it. A re-occurring chapter in the story of his life.

There'd been too many short term odd jobs. He was too easily frustrated. Didn't do authority well. To quick to strike out. Physically abusive Father. Taught him superior strength won. Hit for being ignorant. Beaten for stupidity. Spineless Mother. Physically dominated. Mentally over-powered. She should've divorced him early on. After the first or second beating. Surely after the third. Didn't have the courage. Five kids later it was too late. Give in. Give up. That became her life sentence. No parole in sight.

Pissed him off thinking about it. Restless came over him. Clenched jaw. Gritted teeth. The anger for it and the anger for all of it kept him from feeling sorry for himself. He shifted. Shit! The elevator started to groan. Somewhere along the way his life had started to go wrong. The point where and when it did, unremembered and long forgotten.

Forty-five now with at least a half dozen or so priors. There was a room without a view waiting for him. Reservation at the "Graybar Hotel" for Albert Tooms. Three squares a day. Community showers. Keep your back to the wall. Eyes up. Meet every hard look with a harder one. He wasn't prey. He wasn't weak. He wasn't a "catcher". Served "extra time" proving it. The "hole" wasn't pleasant but the message was delivered. Don't fuck with me 'cause I'll outlast you.

Sitting up now. Legs swung over the side of the bed. Stared at the wall. Don't dwell. Live for the day. Tomorrow will come either way.

A brand new eight inch buck knife lay on the nightstand next to the bed. The Edge had been right. Walk into any Army Surplus. Walk out with a new blade. No questions. No paperwork. No nothing. His plan, get rid of the witness. That bitch from the store. What did the lawyer say her name was? Natalie? No. Russian sounding. Natasha! That was it.

He had her address from the P.D.'s file. A leery grin started. She'd been a good citizen. Stepped up. Put the finger on him. Too bad for her. He was going to put more than a finger on her. He planned on putting his new blade on her. Watch her body spasm. Watch her die.

Since his escape from the stupid cop who got too close while escorting him to the transport van, his nights had been busy. Spent between keeping an eye on the woman's house while addressing his financial needs. Even being on the lamb, money hadn't been too hard to come by.

Following drunks leaving bars to their cars in dimly lit parking lots really wasn't that hard. One hand pushing the back of their head face down into the pavement while they blubbered incoherently. Digging in their pockets for wallets, loose bills and plastic.

He had lightweight connections. Sold the Credit cards. Sold the Social Security numbers. Followed Edge's advice. Sold the cop's gun. Three hundred. Not a bad score. It was bottom rung survival. Credit Cards brought a hundred. Socials brought fifty. Fifteen hundred dollars last count. Mostly five's and ten's. A lot of singles. Throw in some twenties. Four hundreds. Half a dozen fifties. Paid for the Hotel room. Paid for food. He was a good survivor. He was a good predator. He knew how to spot the weak. Single them out. Move in with stealth. He was in his third stolen ride. Parked a block away. A.D.D. kicked in.

There was a debt he had to call. When it came to doing time because of her, he wasn't going to wait long. Didn't have a lot of patience. He could wait a little bit if he had to. She was the only witness. No testimony meant no jail time. Grab her. Some place quiet. Remote. He knew about the cop boyfriend. Knew he might be a problem but nothing he couldn't deal with. He'd dealt with one already. Incompetent assholes. He chuckled. Snatch the bitch then get rid of her. Close her eyes. Close her mouth for good.

TWELVE

Natasha had seen some iffy people at Earls. Rednecks were abundant even in Wenatchee. Both the male and female variety. Wannabe James Bond types. They all gave her the eye. Gave her whatever game they could conjure up. She gave them all disdainful looks. Rated them all a minus on the evolutionary scale. Earl being one of the few that functioned like a normal human.

There was however one guy. Came in infrequently. Definitely not a local. Had that Al Pacino Godfather look. Always well groomed. Smelled good. Not like the locals whose "eau de fragrance" was an aromatic cloud of beer breath and sweat that followed them around. Nice haircut. Always in dark glasses. Sporty dresser. Casual slacks. Pastel, open neck shirts in muted colors. Tailored looking sports coats always open. Loafers. Rolex and pinky rings. An easy way about him. A quiet softness in a hard body. Discreetly threatening. When she asked Earl about him Earl got nervous. Shook his head.

"I don't know him from nothing." Was his reply when she mentioned him. "You don't know him from nothing either." He'd added with a squinty-eyed shake of the head. "Won't come to no good. Leave it alone." Then turned, walked away. Conversation over.

So for now, this part of her "new career" became a waiting game. Watching. She spent a couple of hours a day sitting in the Monte waiting for "sporty" to show up. A week into it. She spotted him. Drove up in a shiny, black Mustang. Windows tinted way too dark to be legal. She was sure it was a ticketable offense. Connections notwithstanding.

Watched him get out. Smooth like Ryan. More fluid. Moved easily to the trunk. Pulled out a small, hand gun case. Heading for the front door. She was moving. Fifteen feet behind him. Carrying her own case in hand.

It was quiet inside Earl's. Subdued. Not many customers. Picked up a couple boxes of ammo. They came with a wary eye from Earl. No extra charge. Followed Sporty downstairs to the shooting range. Kept a discreet distance. Figured he knew anyway. Nobody else around. Just the two of them. She put three shooting stalls in-between. Pulled her Glock .40 from the hard, black plastic carry case. Fifty rounds on the counter. Enough to heat the barrel. Ears on.

She started with the target at fifteen feet. Emptied one fifteen round clip. One flyer. A neck shot. The rest in her now usual five inch pattern. Run the target to twenty-five feet. Concentrating. Focused. One more clip. No flyers. Same five inch pattern. Thirty rounds in a five inch pattern means you're shooting through a hole in the target. There's no paper left. The target shifts ever so slightly from the breeze created by the rounds whistling through the center hole.

A gentle tap on her shoulder. Startled. She jumped. Heart pounding. Adrenalin slathered the edges of her tongue. Turned. Well, well, well. Sporty. His ear covers were hanging around his neck. She laid the Glock down beside the extra rounds on the small counter in front of her. Pulled off her ears. Let them hang around her neck. Two of a kind.

"Hey." She said. Her eyes said wary. His penetrating.

"You shoot o.k." He remarked. Up close she could see what Earl had meant about knowing nothing. Even with peppermint breath, Sporty gave off dangerous. Helped along by his sparkling white, shark-tooth smile.

"Go ahead." She said through tight lips. "Finish it."

He gave her confused. "Finish it?"

"Ya, you know finish the thought." She gave him Command Presence. He held his ground. "I shoot o.k. For a girl. Right? Isn't that where you were going?"

He laughed. One of those head tilted back guffaws. When it settled, he shook his head.

"Not at all young lady. Not at all." His face went hard. Serious. Scary. "You shoot o.k. for a girl, a man, a gorilla, a heavy hitter, whomever. I give you a compliment. You get defensive." He took a step back. Gave her a slow once over. Appraising. "Do you give your man the same defensive crap and he doesn't care or do you not have a man?"

Command Presence. Keep it up. "Maybe I over-reacted. Thanks for the compliment." Dismissed the question about having a man. She figured he knew before he asked anyway. She started reaching her hands up. Ready to put her ears back on. Give him indifference. See how he responds.

He reached out. Put a hand on her left wrist. Felt heavy. Felt strong. Stopped the ears from going into place. "When you're done," he paused, "maybe you'll let me buy you a drink at the bar across the street?" He didn't do puppy-dog. Probably hasn't ever tried. He looked like the kind of man who got what he wanted by asking. Then taking. No puppies allowed.

She removed his right hand from her wrist with her right. "Ya. Maybe." She slipped her ears back in place. Popped out the empty mag' and slapped a full one in the gun butt. Chambered a round. Looked to see if Sporty had his ears on. Saw his back walking away. Ryan had a better ass. Turned to the target and put fifteen in. Four flyers. The five inch pattern? Gone. The size of the hole in the center mass didn't change. Eleven rounds stacked can do that.

Twenty minutes later. She hadn't notice him leave. Wasn't surprised. Fluid smooth can do that. She walked to the front door. Past a hard, narrow-eyed look from Earl. Again no charge. She gave him a shoulder shrug. Her life was hers. She spotted Sporty waiting. Leaning. Butt up against the driver's door. The 'Stang suited him. She walked. Stopped two feet in front. Feet shoulder width. Command Presence. He licked his lips.

"So little lady, who the fuck are you?" He asked. Suspicious. Sly smile. Slight grin. Eyelids squinted. Giving penetrating.

She gave him "who me?" with scrunched shoulders. Dug out a cigarette. He lit it. Fast. "No one really." She replied. "A woman who likes to shoot. That's about it." She took a full hit. Tilted her head, blew the smoke out at seventy degrees. Show him your neck. Men like women's necks. Women like men who like women's necks. "Relaxes me. I think of it as stress relief. Anger management."

He chuckles. "Stress relief. Right." He turns his head towards the bar across the street. Aptly enough the neon sign said "Shooters". Talk about irony. "One for the road?"

She hesitates. Another hit. More smoke. Straight across. "One drink. I buy my own. I drink what I want." She gave him determined.

"Jesus lady lighten up huh?" Chuckles quietly. Hands jammed into his pockets. "I'm not the Spanish Inquisition for Christ's sake." Turned his head. Quick right. Quick left. Traffic was light. He did a lazy jaunt across two lanes. She stood and watched. Thought. Time to decide. I can blow this off or follow through.

She needed what she figured he could get her. She didn't want secrets from Ryan. On this adventure, he was better off not knowing. For now. The butt got tossed. Quick look left. Quick look right. Lazy sprint across two lanes.

He was at the bar. Deep breath. Blow it slow. Take the stool next to him. Bartender looks at Sporty. Bartender looks at Nat. Sporty nods. Bartender stands in front of her. Raised eyebrows give her a question.

"Perrier in a tall glass. Crushed ice with a twist. Lemon. Not lime."

Bartender looks dubious. Walks away. She digs her pocketbook out drops a ten on the bar. Spins the ashtray. Sporty hasn't looked her way yet. Talks into the mirror behind the bar.

"So. You came." His hands rotate the whiskey glass. A slow, tight circle on the napkin. Looks like a double of something amber.

"Curious." She replies. The bartender is back. Unscrews the top. Pours the Perrier. Takes a small wedge of lemon from a bucket sitting in ice below the bar. Squeezes it into the center of the glass. Hangs the rind from the edge. Walks away.

"What's your name shooter?" Sporty is staring daggers into the mirror. Maybe he's trying to make it crack.

"Natasha." She answers. Raises the glass. Drinks a third. Shooting makes you thirsty.

"What? Russian? Or something?"

"Something." Sets the condensating glass on the napkin. Digs for a cigarette. Sporty is fast again.

"One of the few bars you can still smoke in." He remarks. The mirror might be winning.

"Gets my vote." She replies turning the glass slowly on her napkin. Two of a kind.

"So besides shooting the hell out of that .40 and drinking Perrier with a twist, what is that you do shooter?" She could feel him turn. The mirror won that round.

She waited. Took a hit. Blew it at the mirror. So far mirror abuse hasn't been classified as a crime. Yet. "I guess you could say I'm no longer riding on the Merry-go-'round." A line from a John Lennon song. Made her smile. She liked Lennon. Yoko? Whatever. "Yourself?"

Turns all the way this time. Keeps his right hand on the glass. Eye lock. Penetrating. She gave him nothing. Gave the mirror her best shot. She might have a chance. "Well, I'm very much riding the ride." Turns the glass slowly. "I can appreciate your skill. Natasha."

He let it roll off his tongue. Made it sound breathy. She felt the Force quiver. Huh? "In fact, I'm in a position to align you with certain individuals who would also appreciate your skills." Waits a beat. "Even reward you for them."

The road was getting bumpy. Potholes. Dips. Blind curves. Yellow flashing lights. Black squiggly lines on yellow signs. Chains required. Slippery when wet. Pick up the drink. Swallow another third. Take a last hit. Abuse the mirror. Crush out the smoke. "Is that the trade you're in Sporty? Supplying skills? Aligning yourself with certain individuals?"

She gave him hard. He didn't acknowledge.

"I get paid very well." Justifying.

"And one day you get paid off." Pick up the glass. Drain it. Did I say shooting makes you thirsty?

He shrugs. "Supposition on your part." Now he lights his own cigarette. I'm not that fast.

"Well let's suppose." She slides off the stool. Leaves the ten on the bar. Expensive Perrier. Lowers her voice, continues. Bartender catches on fast. Locates himself at the furthest point behind the bar from their conversation. "Suppose someone wants to shoot quietly. Discreetly. Not draw any attention. Doesn't have the right, uh, let's say equipment. Where do you think a person might be able to find something like that? You know, for, let's say the forty I've got." She turns facing him now. Face hard, feet shoulder width. The edge of personal space.

"You think I'm the kind of person who can answer that question?" He gives her hard look back with a taste of cold-blooded. She gives calm, dispassionate.

He turns back to the mirror. Some people just don't learn. "You bring me a thousand. "Pauses. "No wait. For you shooter, I'll make you a deal. Five. Three days. Right here. This time." Picks up the whiskey glass. Tilts it seventy degrees. They say women like a strong neck on a man. Puts the glass down quietly. The bartender doesn't move from his distant spot. Not yet. Sporty stands. Gives the bartender a nod. Nod returned. Sporty heads for the door. Natasha watches. Still likes Ryan's ass better. This one carries an element of danger though. She can feel her heart in her chest.

The door opens. Bright sunlight. The door closes. Nat gives the bartender curious. He gives her relieved. She understands. She works on wearing a tight grin. Makes it. She'll be back in three days. Five hundred in her purse. Her life just made a dramatic change. You gotta love the adrenalin. The moist palms. The barely perceptible quiver in the fingers. The heavy sigh. Time to go. She headed for the door, deep thoughts wrinkling her brow.

THIRTEEN

Monday came. That Monday. The Justice System would finally rear its ugly head. It was all formality. I showed. Ryan showed. Prosecutor. Public defender. Judge. Bailiffs. Court reporter. Gallery members who sacrificed their watching daytime re-runs of "Let's Make A Deal". We were all there.

"All rise." Came the booming voice from the over six foot, burly looking court clerk. Shuffling, scraping feet. Judge enters from his concealed door in the wall. Two steps up. Sits. Black leather, high backed chair. Executive style. Matching black robe. Very stately.

Crossed arms shading his beer barrel chest. "Be seated." Clerk bellows. More scraping and shuffling feet. The Judge shuffles manila files. Paperwork whispers. Reading glasses come out. Perched on the of his nose, he speaks. Doesn't need a mic. Big voices seem to be a prerequisite for Courtroom employment.

"In the case of the State versus Emilio Santori. Are we ready to proceed?" Glances at the Prosecutor's table.

Lyle Hawthorne rises. Clean and tight as usual. "State is ready your Honor." Dark blue suit. Red power tie. Judge nods, turns to the Defense table. Gives him penetrating.

"Is the Defense ready?"

Public Defender stands. Drops his head giving an "Oh shit!" look. Leans his weight forward. Both hands resting against the edge of the table. "Oh shit" turns to sheepish.

"Uh, Your Honor Defense has a minor problem." Sucks in a fresh breath of air.

Judge gives hard. "Did you not have sufficient time to prepare your case?"

"Uh, time to prepare doesn't seem to be the problem Your Honor." His head and eyes raise. He waits. Takes a breath. Blows it out. "The problem seems to be the lack of a Defendant."

"Your Defendant is not present?" Blustery. Booming with conviction. "Is he ill?"

"Uh, I uh, can't say Your Honor."

"Well then enlighten me Counsel. What can you say? Let's start with where the hell is he?" Formality seems to be leaving the Judges vocabulary.

Public Defender appears to be wilting. "Uh, well, uh, I, uh, don't know Your Honor. He was notified of the court date at our last meeting. I fully expected him to be here."

Judge now looking frumpy on top of sounding pissy. Frustration rearing its ugly head. Decorum has, like Mr. Santori, disappeared. Can't be found. "And when prey tell was that last meeting Counselor?"

"Uh, I uh, at the arraignment."

Judge transitions from frumpy to glowering. "You mean to tell me you haven't consulted with your client since the arraignment?"

The Public Defender drops his gaze to the table. Visibly squirming. Shakes his head. Mumbles under his breath. Searching. No answers magically appear on the desk. He opts for the truth. "Uh, no sir. Your Honor."

Judge breathes heavily. The mic is working just fine. Clears his throat. "Bail is revoked." Turns to the clerk. "Issue a bench warrant for the Defendant, uh," eyes shoot to the open file, "Emilio Santori." The manila file folder is closed with a loud flap. The gavel is reached for and a resounding "thunk" echoes throughout the courtroom. "Next case."

We all rise. P.D. probably re-thinking his career choices.

The hall outside of the courtroom is bustling. Lawyers. Tall. Short. Fat. Lean. Three piece suits. Creaseless. Public Defenders. Ill-fitting sports coats in need of a pressing. No color co-ordination. Tasseled Loafers. Defendants. Dressed up as best as they can. Still looking disheveled. Teary-eyed Mothers of Defendants. Witnesses looking wide-eyed at the circus performers surrounding them. A rabble of hushed conversations. Ryan has his face less than a foot from Hawthorne's. Two egos clashing in two bodies standing off to the side of the elevator.

"I friggin' ass told you Lyle." Ryan's giving heat. "I said there'd be a bondsman out there more than happy to own a house for fifty "K." Backs up a step to suck in a fresh lungful of air. "But you said don't worry. He'll be here. He'll be here when we need him." Does a full 360 degree turn. Steps in. "Space Invader". "Well Lyle, you think we might need him? Like right now!"

Lyle's looking pale. Uncomfortable. Would rather be someplace else. Anywhere else if the truth be told. "We'll pick him up." He tries authoritative. It falls flat.

"No Counselor, you won't pick him up. You'll be sitting at home enjoying a nice dinner with your wife. A dinner that I won't be having. Because I'll be out there beating the bushes trying to find him and pick him up. Because if I don't, the length of the plaintiff's life comes into question." Lyle's eyes search and find me.

They say some dog's barks are worse than their bite. In Detective Steve Ryan's case, equality is the rule. He takes a step back. Swivels his head. I'm three feet to his right. Wet blanket ready. If needed. "Let's get out of here." He says evenly. Head swivels back to Hawthorne. Looks Lyle in the eye. "I hate failure. I hate excuses. I hate stupid!" Turns to the shiny aluminum elevator doors. Jams his thumb onto the down arrow button. At some point plastic shatters. Doors whisper open. Amazing.

The heat is obvious. The ride down takes too long. Out through the double glass doors into the early morning. We make it all the way to the sidewalk. Debbie Dallas. Ryan stops. Mumbles. "Damn it!"

Lights. Action. Hands jam into his slacks pockets. D.D. approaches. Purposeful stride. Ryan turns to me. Gives me, uh, tries calm. Close but no cigar. I spot frustrated. Camera rolls.

"Detective Ryan." She strides up. Determined. "How frustrating is it? It's my understanding that you requested a much higher bail."

Ryan's wearing grim. Flashes impatience. "I'm sorry?" Fakes confused.

"Well it seems the District Attorney was, uh, oh let's say maybe less than concerned at the arraignment hearing." Tongue dart. Lips glistening for the close-up. "You know, agreeing to a bail reduction . . ." She lets it trail off. Moves the mic in closer to Ryan's face.

"Hey. That was between the Judge, the D.A. and the P.D." Quick glance back to the front of the courthouse. "I made my recommendation. It was ignored. Now thanks to their poor judgment, the criminal is back on the street." Looks directly into the camera. No tongue dart. Not a glistening lip kind of guy. "But I'll have him back in custody soon enough."

Gives the camera a glare. Eyebrows furrowed with determination. If it was human it would've wilted. He narrows his eyelids. Gives menacing. "You feelin' me Emilio? Keep one eye looking over your shoulder. Watch your six. I'm not far behind." Ryan turns from the camera. Turns from Debbie Dallas. Gives me irritable. "Let's get outta here."

We both start towards the parking lot. Debbie is left holding the mic. Looking flustered. Maybe it's the blonde hair. I let it go. "Hey look." I start. "We'll get 'em. Both of them. Lawnmower Guy and Tooms. One at a time." I give confident. "I've got the forty in my purse. Full mag. Chambered round. I'll be good when it counts. You know that." He's wearing a variation of sullen. Not quite condescension. I dig a smoke out. Light it. He's not fast.

Well sometimes. "You got stuff to do. I'll be at the house for, I don't know, 'til I'm not. I got stuff."

He's wearing concerned. "Well, just keep your toes on. Crap! I mean keep on your toes. Stay alert. Eyes up. Sweep one eighty while you walk. Watch your six. No distractions. There's two assholes out there. Either one or both are looking for you. Either one wants a piece. Don't let your guard down." His head swivels. Left. Right. Behind me. Then behind him. "I've got to get back to the store put a B.O.L.O. out on Santori. Call my cell if you need me." Takes a step in. Steve Ryan, "Space Invader". Quick hug. Step back. Space Invader is not a big fan of p.d.a.

"At the house then. Later." Small smile. Give him calm. Sell it. Turn for the parking lot. My chariot awaits. Could be a top down day. Stop at the bank. Pick up the five. Meet a man at a bar.

*　　　　*　　　　*

The Motel was across town. Close to the interstate. Far from what used to be his house. Emilio was having trouble. Trying to figure out what to do. Up and pacing. Sit and think. Up and pacing. Sit and think. He was wearing out the edge of the bed. Staring at the curtained window beside the door to the room. The man at the Bail Bonds office was very clear about what would happen if Emilio missed his court date. No more bond. No more house.

It was the woman's fault. She was the cause of it all. Her too tight shorts. Making him have thoughts. The thin gauzy see through tops. Making him feel confused. He'd never seen his Mother walking around like that. Without a bra.

He remembered. She wore course feeling pull-over sweaters. Rough, thick fabric that scratched his skin. Never thin. Never almost see through. Full skirts or loose fitting slacks. Never ever saw her naked. One time she caught him peeking. Heated his butt up with a leather belt. Couldn't sit straight for three days. Up and pacing again. He was depressed. No money. No definite future. At least not in this town. Back sitting on the edge of the bed. Had to go somewhere. Where? Away from this place that was for sure. He could feel the heat. Made him edgy.

Head down. Hands holding the sides if his face. Elbows resting on his knees. Thinking. Pissed at the woman. Her fault. Damn, damn, Damn her! Damn her calves. Damn her thighs. Damn her too tight shorts. Damn all of her. Feels a leery grin coming. Stops it. Show some control. Thought change.

Maybe head north. Someplace close to the Canadian border. There were wild places up north not too far from Wenatchee. Remote places where you could disappear. Get swallowed up. Big forests filled with lots of big trees. He looked down at the map beside him. Small towns. Lakes. Rivers.

He spotted a small town by the border. Liked the name. Found a small scratch pad and a tired looking ballpoint pen in the top drawer of the nightstand. Wrote the name on the scratch pad. Ball point was running out of ink. Went over the letters twice. Pressed harder the second time. Looked like it was surrounded by forests. Wilderness. He could come up with a new name. Fifty wasn't too old to be on the run. A vision of the woman slipped back in. He had mental pictures saved. Cut off shorts. Blue jean material gripping her behind. Natasha. He smiled. Silent giggle.

FOURTEEN

Her meeting at the bar with "Sporty" had gone well. Or well enough. Table in the back. Far from the front door. Only three other customers. Sitting at the bar. Taking their shot at trying to stare down the mirror. Earl came by with their drinks. He was clearly concerned about the company she was keeping. Gave her a hard look. No charge. A lot of that going around lately. She gave him "Back off." Gave the paper shopping bag by Sporty's feet a wary, nervous eye.

"It's in the bag." He replied when her eyes came up to his face. "No pun intended."

Her tight grin was meant to look professional. A confident affirmation. Like she knew that. Had done this or something like this before.

"So let me ask." He began. "Not that I'm prying, but who's the lucky guy?" Pause for a sip of his drink. "Assuming of course that a man is going to be on the receiving end of your indiscretion."

Her eyes dropped to her glass. She watched her slender fingers turn it slowly on the napkin. "Who says I'm doing anything indiscreet? Maybe I want to accessorize what I already have." She tried selling nonchalant. He wasn't buying.

Sporty chuckles. His right hand rises slowly. Fingers slide under the lapel, disappearing inside the sports coat. Her breath catches. Their eyes lock. Her tongue darts out. Licks her top lip. No time to go for the gun in her purse. He reads it all.

"You know," he begins, not taking his eyes off hers, "you might think I don't know fuck all about anything." His hand comes out from inside the jacket. Cigarettes and lighter. "Your mistake." Shakes out a cigarette. Grabs it with his lips. Flicks the lighter. Long drag sucked into his lungs. Smoke comes out his mouth when he continues. "You might think your some kind of hot shit broad." Blows the rest of the inhale towards the table. Picks up where he left off. "Just so we're clear. Yes, you are a fine piece of engineering. I'll give you that. Maybe in my younger years I would've been confused. Nervous. You know, how to deal with a good looking woman and all. Let me tell you. I'm forty-eight. I've had the best. I've had the worst." Gives her narrowed eyelid penetrating. "You don't hold a candle to the best. A few significant cuts above the worst." Another long drag.

I sit feeling outclassed. Tongue-lashed. This real professional giving me his taste of reality. Maybe I need it. I wait. "You wanna give me bullshit. You wanna believe I believe it. Your choice." Another pull at the butt. Smoke comes out his mouth giving his words form and substance. "You think it's like putting bullets in paper targets? You think that's how its gonna go? You're stupid." Holds her eyes. Crushes the smoke in the ashtray. "You better have a plan. A damn good plan. A plan so tight anyone trying to decipher it, frontwards, backwards or sideways, gets a monster fucking migraine."

Their eyes haven't unlocked since he began the lecture. Not even when he crushed out the smoke. Did it by feel. She was breathing a little quicker now. Wanted to drop her eyes from his penetration. Didn't want to give him the satisfaction.

She tried bluster. Heart wasn't in it. "I have to sit through this kind of lecture every time we do business?" Not really expecting an answer. Didn't get one. Dropped her eyes to the glass. Picked it up trying not to let her hand shake. Small tremble. Uncontrollable. Drank a third. Acting tough makes you thirsty. He replied with a laugh. More like a bark. One sharp "Ha" that came with a backwards jerk of his head then a smaller side to side head shake.

"You got balls honey. Ya you do." More head shaking then it stops. He's giving her severe. "Most men would look. Once. They'd put some kind of a buffer between me and them. They wouldn't talk. Maybe nod maybe not. You, you start a frigging conversation. Not about nothing. You start a conversation about acquiring a silencer. Big, brass balls honey. Yes indeed." He stands. Looks down at her. Waits. "You got it?"

She breathes out. Big. Hopes he can't tell how much. She pauses. Wondering. Oh fuck! The money damn it. He's waiting. Still looking down. She makes a grab for her purse. She feels slow. Clumsy. Digs inside. Past the gun. Pulls out the envelope. Hands it out to him. He doesn't take it. Her eyes go from the envelope to his face. Back to the envelope. She lays it on the table.

Sporty looks over towards the bartender. Shrugs his shoulders. Raises his arms waist high palms up. Shakes his head. Random thought. She wonders if he gets headaches easily. All the head shaking. He reaches down. Picks it up. Quickly slips it inside his sports coat. Gives her one last narrowed eyelid look. "Good luck Kid." Takes a step. Stops. "'Til we meet again." Then he starts for the door.

She doesn't turn her head to watch. Still working on settling her breathing. Slowing down her thumping heart. Listening to his footsteps retreating. Hears the bar door open. Flash of bright light punches the interior. Listens to the door close. Breathes big. In through her nose. Pursed lips blow it out. Stays sitting at the table. Emotionally spent. Picks up the glass. Drains it.

Condensation on the outside of the glass wets her fingers. Rubs her fingers on her jeans to dry them. Stands. Reaches down. Picks up the paper shopping bag by the rolled over top. Turning she walks with purpose to the bar's front door. Feels the bartender's eyes on her. Keeps her head straight. Doesn't turn her head just breaks through the front door.

Blinking into the bright sunlight, the bar's front door closed with a thud behind her. Quick steps it to the Monte's trunk. Keyed it open. Placed the paper shopping bag inside. Closed the trunk with a bang. Leaning forward, both hands on the trunk, she turned her head and stared at Earls. Had an idea.

She pulled out of Shooters parking lot, drove across the street, pulled into Earls. Time to accessorize the new her. She tried on three or four shoulder rigs. Picked out a leather one with stretchy over-the-shoulder straps. Earl gave her the evil eye. Gave her concerned. Gave her "what are you up to." She gave him "mind your business Earl." She left him shaking his head.

On her way to an Army Surplus. More accessories. Night vision Military binocs. A nice eight inch hunting knife. A calf strap with a leather scabbard. Rather have it and not need it, then wish for it and not have it. Wishes were for young, Elementary School daydreamers. Not tight-lipped women. Especially not tight-lipped women on a mission.

Picked out some black and brown camo fatigues. They came with narrow, twelve inch long, side of the thigh pockets. Velcro flap. Silencer in. Silencer out. Smooth. Grabbed a pair of black hiking boots. Size six. Added a pair of thin, skin tight, black leather gloves. Black watch cap. Out of ideas. Four hundred seventy-five dollars later she sat behind the wheel of the Monte. The trunk held many secrets. A dark spot appeared on her heart. It slowly grew.

     *   *   *

The Monte idled up the driveway. She braked a couple of feet from the garage. It was going on six. Ryan had texted. Would be home by seven. Time enough. Through the side garage door into the hose. Check the fridge. Some veggies. Pound of ground turkey. Still pinkish. Check the cupboard. Wide linguini. There it is. Pasta with veggies, "Newman's Own" sauce. Done in half an hour.

While the pasta was cooking in the pot of boiling water, Natasha was putting her black nylon bag together. The broken up burger was browning in the frying pan, sharing space with broccoli florets, mushrooms and sliced zucchini. The duty bag was stocked. Her supplies packed. She hefted it into the house. Stuck it in the back of the hall closet.

Back in the kitchen. Poured a glass of Merlot. Took it into the living room. Sitting at last, she rested her head against the back of the couch. Her mind drifting. The wine glass sitting half full on the coffee table. She would make Lawnmower guy pay. See how he liked a little role reversal. See how he liked being tied to a chair. No cheeseburgers. No fries. No nothing. She was running the movie in her head when the front door opened. Ryan.

"Honey I'm home." He said it with a chuckle. Her head came off the back of the couch when she heard the front door. Smiled at his entry. Grinned at his greeting.

"I'm here." She said from the couch.

Ryan turned right from the entry. Sauntered into the living room. His eyes went from Nat's face to the half drunk glass of wine. He dropped onto the couch beside her. "Smells good."

She dropped her right hand onto his left thigh. Leaned across. Put her lips on his. Tasted salty. Tasted good. "I know how to keep a man happy." Gave him bedroom eyes. He smiled back.

"Yes you do." He replied. Changed subjects. "Man what piece of crap day." He reached down picked up her glass. Took a mouthful. Glass back on the coffee table. Big swallow. "Got men running sideways trying to track down Albert. Trying to track Santori. Man hours out with not much to show." Heavy sigh. Leans back into the couch. "Cap' wants results. Said so on the phone before I bailed on the day. I assured him we, my guys and me, were all on the same page about that. He grunted and hung up."

She gives concerned. "You'll get there honey. You usually do." She rises. "Gotta get the food out. You hungry?" Starts for the kitchen

"Like a wolf." He replies rising. "Need help?" He starts to follow.

"Serving in the kitchen. Grab a plate and help yourself."

It was as good as it had smelled. Two empty plates in the drip rack proved it. By the time they were done with kitchen clean-up, it was time to shower with a friend and spend some together time under the sheets.

Three o' clock A.M. She sat in the chair at the writing desk. Across the room from the bed. Watching him sleep. Listening to him breathe. The smoke trail from her cigarette drifted silently up to the ceiling. The lovemaking had been long. Had been passionate. Sweaty. Fulfilling.

She stared at his shadowy form. She knew tomorrow would be the day. The day of departure. She didn't want to piss him off. Keeping a secret this big could bring their relationship crashing down. It could flame out. That scared her. She crushed out the smoke. Glided softly across the carpeted floor to the bed. Slipped under the sheets. Lay on her side facing him. Smelled him. Wallowed in the comfort. Let the feeling of security envelope her. Felt a tear form in her eye and run silently down her cheek.

FIFTEEN

Empty house. Sitting alone at the computer, Ryan gone by a couple hours. Freshly filled coffee cup on the desk. Google maps on the computer. Santori's house under the arrow. The hub. Would he go back? She wasn't sure. She guessed probably not. Stupid but not that. If not there, where? She didn't think he'd go too far. Everyone likes familiarity.

She first heard the acronym at Law School. Came up again at B.F.D. R.E.P.O.B. "Repeated Patterns of Behavior." We all like to travel the same streets. Eat at the same restaurants. Frequent the same convenience stores. Humans are habitual. She'd give him three miles. The house at the hub. Copy. Paste. Print. She held the map. Drew a dark circle. Six mile diameter. Three mile radius every direction from the house. She felt a tactile rush. Tongue dart. Not for a lip glistening close-up but for senses prickling.

There were twelve or so Motels. Six Hotels. A day's work. Maybe a day and a half. Take some time to eat. Make it like the business it was. Keep it relaxed and professional. Keep it methodical.

The file on Ryan's desk didn't show any relatives in the area. Ryan's file had a picture. She scanned it. Printed two dozen copies. Started a "go pile" on the couch by the front door. Two bottles of water. Half a dozen Granola bars. Two or three fifteen round clips. A couple sets of hand cuffs. Pepper Spray. A new bag of sixteen inch zip ties. Grabbed her new black, nylon "Duty Bag" courtesy the Army Surplus store from the hall closet. She stopped. Breathe. Slow down. Think. She was at the point of no return. You start this mission, there's no going back. No changing your mind half way in.

She could feel her palms moistening up. Wiped them on the sides of her fatigues. Toss everything in the bag. Walk to the Monte. Key in the trunk lock. Bag in the trunk. Back inside. Write a quick note. She didn't know how long it would take but for now Ryan mustn't know. She didn't want to compromise his job or his integrity.

She didn't figure he'd support her explanation. "Ya, I'm going after Lawnmower guy. My intentions are to hunt him down, torture him. Like he did me. Then kill him. Kill him like the vermin he is." It wouldn't sit well with an Officer of the Law. Didn't want his O.C.D. help anyway. Emilio's debt was hers to collect. Not him. He could have Albert. They had history.

She wrote quickly on a sticky pad. "Too much stress. Don't feel safe here. Going for a drive. Will call when I get there." Stuck it on the front of the T.V. Left the foyer light on. Pulled the front door closed. Keyed the dead bolt. It was time to get on the road. Her plan was simple. She would hit the motels closest to his house first. Then expand the circle. How hard could it possibly be?

*   *   *

Albert sat watching. Half a block away. Chewing on a stick of beef jerky. The stolen, faded tan, Chevy pickup he sat in was inconspicuous. Dissolved into the background. Like a black and white parked twenty yards from an intersection looking for stop sign "rollers". He could see she was up to something. Watched her toss a black bag in the trunk. Could'a been heavy. Too far away to tell. He was out of patience. He needed to make his move.

She slid behind the wheel closed the driver's door. He fired up the truck. Watched her pull away from the curb. He jerked the shifter out of park. Eased out onto the street. Stalking mode. Keep your distance, be unobvious he told himself.

Albert was confused. You could debate whether there were forty something, fifty or even fifty-one cards in his mental deck. He would adamantly assure you there were at least fifty-two. Insist there were quite possibly fifty-three. That statement making the vote for less than fifty-two even more credible. Not to mention the last time he was picked up, he was trying to break into a Laundromat. Point made.

She'd drove normally. Keeping to the speed limit, turn signals and all. He followed her lead. Kept his "stalking" distance. They ended up all the way across town. East side. Not far from Route 97. He watched her pull into the "Just Right Motel". A cartoon rendition of a baby bear wearing a nightcap, adorned a plastic electric sign sitting on the roof above the office. He smiled. This was perfect. She couldn't be more vulnerable. He'd wait to see which room she went in. Then tonight. Darkness. He would be in his element. Darkness was his friend.

Slowing down for the turn into the driveway, Albert pulled into a slot. Fifteen or twenty feet from her car. It was the most distance he could create. Small parking lot. He slunk down. Three or four cars between them.

She walked into the Motel Office. Carrying a piece of paper or something in her hand. He watched through his front window into the Office window.

She put what she was carrying on the counter. The lady behind the counter looked down, said something. At least her lips were moving. She looked down again at whatever it was the woman was showing her. Shook her head. Albert read her lips. "Sorry." She mouthed. Heart beating, he watched her walk back and slide into her car.

She picked up a yellow legal pad. Looked for a second or two. Dropped it. Started backing out. What the hell? He dropped his chin. Slunked down further. Made himself small. Waited. Watched. One and one wasn't making two. Now where?

He caught up to her at the next light. One car between them. Three blocks down. Pulls into the "Sleep Tight Motel". Albert was more confused than before. What the hell was she doing? Waste of gas comparing room rates this way. Or what? What did she show the lady at the last place?

Same deal again. Park by the office. Albert parked a few cars away. Waited until she was inside. Slithered out of the stolen truck. Steady eye on the office. Up against her passenger door. Jerk the handle. Locked. Glance at the office. Still good. Glance at the passenger seat. Legal pad with addresses. Pile of 8 x 10's. Some guy.

Slither back to the truck. Close the door quietly. His brain was an unmatched Rubik's cube. He twisted it. Turned it around. All he came up with was huh? Bit his lower lip. Why? Who was the guy? Friend? Relative?

Two and a half hours later. They'd hit Two discount hotels. Six or eight motels. He'd lost count. He needed to pee. His stomach was rumbling. Seven o'clock coffee and granola bar was a long time ago. His watch said five. He wondered when she was going to go back to the house. He'd seen the Detective's car. Parked in the driveway. Usually worked late. There'd be time. If she hurried. When the hell would she be done with whatever the hell she was doing?

Five thirty. She sat at a table by the window. Staring out. Sipping coffee. She wondered where the hell Lawnmower guy was. She summoned up some grit. Summoned a little determination.

"Ready?" The waitress suddenly appeared. Stood waiting. Pen poised. Hovering over her order pad.

"Uh, ya. Salmon steak. Green beans, carrots, mashed potatoes and refill the coffee please." Half smile.

The waitress nodded. Wrote. Smiled. Left.

Two pages on the legal pad. She was resolute. Check marks beside a lot of the names. West side was done. Three or four stops on the south side of the circle. Hunger came. Spotted the coffee shop. As soon as her eyes landed on it she got hungrier. It looked like it would work.

"Just Like Home". Never been there before. Placard with a red letter "A" rating in the window looked promising. At least she wouldn't get food poisoning. Coming back from the bathroom. Met the waitress at the table. Smiled a thank you. The food looked good. Salmon Steak was about the right color. Veggies looked green. Always a good sign. Mashed potatoes. How do you screw up mashed potatoes? Coffee smelled comforting.

She wondered about Ryan. Missed his smell. Missed him. Maybe a call? He'd grill her. Where? What? Why? The whole nine yards. Tell her to forget about it. Let him do his job. He'd take care of it. Come home. She shook her head. Maybe when she had a location for Santori pinned down. Then maybe not.

What was the point of doing all the prep work? The secrets in the trunk? She'd lose the adrenalin rush. She was entitled damn it! Her eyes got hard. Chewing got rigid. Stirring sugar in the coffee got faster. Green beans got stabbed. Wasn't their fault. Heavy sigh. Swallow. Reach for the coffee. She felt a renewed sense of determination. A dish best served hot.

*   *   *

Albert watched from across the street. Parking lot of "The Burger Joint". Aptly named. Some non-descript block of red bricks and tinted glass. Serving their version of fast food. Had a bathroom that had come just in time. Chocolate shake. Chili cheeseburger with fries. The cab of the truck faced the "Just Like Home" restaurant. He could pick her out at a table by the window. In his mind, her testimony rose up like a roadblock. A barrier between him and his freedom. He wasn't going back to the slammer. Not for her. Not for anyone. Not if he had anything to say about it. He'd

"Dillinger" his way to the next life. Go out in a hail of bullets.

Albert wasn't a big believer in destiny. Life was what you made of it. No excuses. No apologies. When you've lived the life that he'd lived, the end was not going to be a white picket fence around a three bedroom house in the 'burbs. He chewed and drank. Tossed the trash on the floor. Keep an eye on the woman. Took a glance in the side view mirror. Saw the black and white pull in. Twenty yards. Froze him. Shit! Damn! Damn! Swallowed before chewing. Hard lump of burger in the back of his throat. His eyes watering, he held his breath. Heart thudding.

Two of them. Linebacker types. Why were cops always so big? Why were they always looking around? The front door of the Burger Joint called. They start for the door. First guy pulls it open. Holds it for the second guy. First guy looks around. Again! Albert feels his eyes. The stolen truck. Shit! Damn! Damn! Albert waited. Brow starting to sweat. Body feels clammy. First cop says something to the second cop. Second cop turns his head. Albert's gut is getting tighter. No doubt there was a B.O.L.O. on the truck. Were they good cops? Maybe. Just putting in time? Debatable.

Albert lifted his arm slowly. Full stealth. Fingers reach for the ignition. Keys are waiting. If they make the truck, step his way . . . Quick glance for an escape route. He'd drive right over the sidewalk. Cross four lanes. Dodge oncoming cars. Head for the side street. Dump the truck. Run through yards. Front and back. Gotta get distance from the pursuers.

Second guy talks into his shoulder mic. First guy lets the front door close. Click. Slow key turn. First cop laughs. Albert lets a breath out. Second cop smiles, pulls the front door open. Albert swallows the lump. Finger tension on the ignition key relaxes. First cop walks inside. Second cop follows. Click. Ignition key turns back. Front door closes. Albert breathes softly in and out. Shakes his head slowly side to side. Picks up the shake. Sip through the straw washes the taste of adrenalin from his mouth. Uses the napkins to wipe the accumulated sweat from his forehead and face. Eyes back on the restaurant. Reconnect with the woman.

      *   *   *

Natasha dropped a five and a couple of singles on the table. The waitress had to live. Minimum wage is a bitch to pay the rent on. She stopped by the front door, paid the check. Grabbed a mint from the bowl by the register. Stepped outside. Front door whooshed closed behind her. Getting late in the day. She'd burned an hour eating. Lawnmower guy was another hour further away from her.

Stood outside the front door. Took a deep breath. Felt re-charged. Picked out the black and white in the parking lot across the street. She didn't miss much. Missed the tan Ford Pick-up. Missed the guy behind the wheel. So would anyone else. Black and whites with light bars on the roof stood out. Non-descript tan pick-ups don't.

She sat in the Monte. Yellow legal pad still had a few unchecked motels. One cheap sounding hotel. Couple more hours. Maybe. Her plan had to work. It had to. There were no alternatives. At least not right now. He had to be out there. Laying low.

Cell went off. Looked at the display. Ryan. Two beats went by. Three. To answer or not to answer. Heavy sigh. She let it go to message. Fired up the Monte, pulled out onto the street. Had a good idea where the next motel was. Ten minutes away. Didn't notice the tan pick-up. Didn't see it slide in behind her four cars back.

      *   *   *

Albert watched. Saw her stand in front of the restaurant. This time he turned the key all the way. She was on the move. In a couple minutes they were on the street. He kept her in sight from four cars back. Cops were a faded memory. He needed new wheels. The stolen truck was stressing him out.

He followed her over to Worthen Street. Couple of blocks from the Columbia River. Saw her turn into another Motel. Muttered profanities out loud buttoned by a "What the Hell?"

The "River View Suites" was an "L" shaped, two storey building with a small parking lot. Enough for ten maybe fifteen cars. He parked in the street with a view of the office. Same routine as the others. Park her car. Get out. Take what he now knew was the eight by ten picture into the office. Then it all changed.

The woman behind the counter nodded. Even from where he sat he could see Natasha's body go rigid. The woman behind the counter lips moved. She shook her head.

He watched Natasha open her purse. Reach inside. Billfold came out. A bill was placed on the counter. No one moved. The counter-woman shook her head again. Another bill was added. The woman behind the counter blinked. She looked edgy. Her head swiveled. She looked around. Another bill placed on top of the other two.

Albert couldn't see what denomination the bills were from where he sat. Three was a lot. Probably not five's. Maybe ten's. If they were twenties Albert would've caved. For sixty bucks he would've given up the goods on his own Mother with a wink and a nod.

The woman caved. Pulled out some kind of book. Ran her finger over a page. Albert watched her lips move. Natasha nodded her head. The woman turned. Took something off a shelf. Gave her what looked like a key fob. Natasha hurried out the office door. Quick-stepped to a unit on the long side of the "L".

*   *   *

Natasha was well into the routine at this point. Grab a picture of Santori. Slide out the driver's door.

Make nice with whoever the Manager was. Show the picture. "Have you seen this man? O.K. thanks." Back to the car. Head to the next stop. This one was the same routine. Up until the part about "have you seen this man?" The woman had nodded. Natasha's heart stopped. Her breath caught. Couldn't swallow. "Is he still here?" She asked. Her blood pressure jumped. Her heart felt like it skipped.

"I'm sorry. Who did you say you were?" The woman questioned. "Are you a relative?"

"Oh, uh, no. Just a friend." She lied. Her eyes dropped down to the picture. You gotta be good to straight out lie to someone while you look them in the eye. She was out of practice. Her eyes raised back up to the woman's face. Stopping along the way to read the name tag pinned to the woman's left breast pocket.

"Listen Trudy, it's really very important that I find this friend of mine." She opened her purse. Dug past the gun. Pulled out her billfold. Pulled out a ten. Laid it on the picture. "I'm not here to make trouble for you. Is this man still here?" She asked again.

This time Trudy didn't speak. Shook her head slowly from side to side. "Can you tell me what room he stayed in when he was here?" Trudy soldiered up. Going for stoic. Would've made a good candidate for a Buckingham Palace guard. Natasha dropped her gaze to her billfold. Pulled another ten out. Laid it on top of the first one. Raised her eyes. Gave her steely-eyed. "Do you remember what room he stayed in?"

"Room seven." Trudy was working class. She showed up every day. Made sure the coffee pot on the table in the lounge area off the check-in counter was full and fresh every morning. Bought a dozen do-nuts to go with the coffee. Her own money. The asshole owner, Bob Wilson, never said a word about it. Not so much as a thank you or even a nod of thanks.

"You think I could get the key to that room Trudy?" Natasha held her gaze. Command Presence. Trudy licked her lips. Looked down at the two tens laying on top of the photo. The man was gone. Left early this morning. What harm could it do?

She watched another ten appear from Natasha's billfold. Watched as it was laid down on top of the other two. Thirty dollars. That was almost two weeks' worth of gas back and forth to work. Thirty dollars could take her to dinner, a movie and still have a few dollars left over. Her resistance left like a Lear jet rocketing down a runway.

Trudy sighed. Turned to a rack of cubby holes hanging on the wall to her right. The key for number seven was right where it was supposed to be. Between cubby six and eight. She stared at it. Waiting for . . . Her arm raised. Her hand reached. Jittery fingers gripped the key. Trudy turned back to face the woman on the other side of the counter. Laid the key to number seven on the counter beside the three tens.

Watched as her hand crept over. Slid the three ten dollar bills off the counter. Slipped them into the back pocket of her jeans. Raised her head to look this woman in the eye. "The room hasn't been cleaned yet." She said quietly. Her cheeks were a little flushed. No doubt embarrassed by her transgression.

"That's o.k. In fact it's better if it hasn't." Natasha was breaking at the bit to get into the room. The fact that it hadn't been cleaned was like Beethoven's ninth symphony playing in her ears. She picked up the key. "Thanks Trudy." Started for the door. "I appreciate your help."

Natasha quickstepped out the front door like she had a plane to catch. This wasn't exactly what she wanted but it was the next best thing. Better to be sniffing at a warm trail than lost in the darkness of a cold one.

The tan pick-up parked in the street went unnoticed. The fact that it had been lingering in her peripheral vision since she started her quest earlier this morning didn't register. She was tunnel-visioned.

The numbers on the individual units started at "1" from the office, going up along the long leg of the "L". Number seven was in the corner. The skin on her body was moist with anticipation. She fumbled the key into the lock. Turned it. Pushed the door open. Reached for the wall switch.

The smell hit her first. Smothered her face. Old sweat. Ripe. Like the inside of a jar of pickles. She walked fully into the room. Closed the door behind her. Locked it. Took it all in. The unmade bed. The overflowing trash can. Fast food wrappers. The bedside table. The small writing desk against the opposite wall with a hard backed chair.

Her head was on a slow swivel. Eyes stopping on individual items. Trash can. Bed. Empty closet, door open. Sliding glass door. Small round ice cream table. Three chairs. Small kitchenette. Microwave on a short counter. Couple of cupboard doors. Another step brought her to the center of the room. Where to start she thought. Where to start.

She started with the dark brown, two foot tall, metal trash can. Took it into the middle of the room. Turned it upside down. Smelled bad. Couldn't make the room smell any worse. Used the toe of her shoe to move stuff around. Didn't know what she was looking for. Food wrappers. Receipts for fast food. Soda cans. Nothing caught her eye. Nothing spoke to her.

Moved to the bedside end table. Older fake brass table lamp. The shade was probably white at one time. Off color shade of dusty beige now. It sat on a two drawer dark wood nightstand. Brass colored handles shaped like a smile looked up at her. She didn't return it. The closer she got the worse the smell. The stink was coming from the bed. Jesus! Didn't this guy ever shower?

The bedside phone on the nightstand stared up at her. She stared back. There wasn't any ethereal communication. Time slipped by in seconds. Think. Think. What would her Dad do? What would Ryan do? Against her better judgment she sat her purse on the bed. Hoping there wouldn't be any bug or disease transfer from the sheets. Dug around inside for a tissue. Don't leave prints. Where did that come from? She wasn't violating a crime scene.

Used the tissue to grab the handle on the top drawer. Pulled. The drawer stuck for a second then slid open. Unremarkable. Bible. Scratch pad with the Motel's name and logo across the top. Number 2 pencil. Used. Nothing else. Closed the top drawer, pulled open the bottom. Empty. Thinking. Thinking. Wearing thoughtful. When you're on the run you travel light. Not much to carry. That means not much to leave behind.

Back to the trash pile. The rising aroma adding to the ambient smell in the room. Toe it around some more. Pointless. Nothing there. Thoughtful left her face replaced by frustrating impatience. It knitted her eyebrows. Another eye scan of the room.

The kitchenette had a sink, a microwave sitting on a short, three foot long counter. A half fridge. Two drawers in the counter. Two cupboard doors above the micro. Five minutes later, having gone through it all, she was no further ahead. The drawers under the counter were empty, sharing their lack of booty with the cupboards.

She walked towards the partially open floor to ceiling curtains in front of a sliding glass door. They opened to an iron railing enclosed terrace. Small B.B. Que. Nothing there. She turned back to the inside of the room. Eyes darting. Front door. Bed. Nightstand. Phone. Closed drawers. Phone. Scratch pad. Closed drawers. Something percolated in her brain. Why?

Subconscious nibbling at the conscious. Leave it. Walk to the bathroom.

Shower with a curtain. At some point white, now stained with soap scum no design. Thinking. Thinking. Did designs raise the price of shower curtains? Random thought. Half closed. Glance around the curtain. Small shampoo. Even smaller soap. Random thought. How could the room smell so bad?   Rust stained toilet bowl. Lid up. Towels were still damp. Damn it! Missed him by . . . . Shook her head in frustration.

Back into the main room. Trash still on the floor. Bed still unmade. Phone still on the nightstand. She moved closer to it. Tissue left by the phone from before. Use it to open the drawer again. What was nibbling at her? Bible. Scratch pad. Number two pencil.

Pick up the scratch pad. Stared at it. There were faint indentations on the top page. Angle it into the light coming from the terrace. She smiled. It was corny. She'd seen it on second and third rate T.V. cop shows. What the hell. Why not? What did she have to lose?

Pencil in hand, she walked. Stopped by the glass slider. Turned the pencil sideways so the side of the lead tip lay against the pad. Light strokes over the indentations. Letters first. Then words. "You've got to be kidding." She mumbled. "No friggin' way."

     *   *   *

Albert sat in the pick-up staring at the door to room seven and wondered. What the hell was she doing? She'd been in there a long time. If he could get over to the room without being seen by the woman behind the counter in the office, this would be the perfect place. They would never be able to tie him to this random motel. Never be able to tie him to the body inside. The damn counter woman was glued in place. Standing there. Head turned, staring at the same door Albert was keeping watch on. The same door that now flung open.

Albert watched the woman hot-step it to her car. She jerked open the driver's side door. Pulled it closed so fast she about closed it on her left foot. Engine fired. Lurched back. Tire chirps on the parking lot pavement. The Monte bolted forward towards the street.

The truck's ignition key turned. The engine turned over. Albert shifted the lever into drive. Took off after the quickly accelerating car. She wasn't wasting any time. Blew through lights as they changed from yellow to red. Albert was doing his best to keep her in sight. He couldn't draw that kind of attention. Not in a stolen truck. He cursed his inability to keep up with her. Slammed his palm against the steering wheel. All he could do was keep an eye on her. The last glimpse he got were her taillights turning onto North Wenatchee Avenue.

"Now where?" He hollered at the front windshield. "Damn it! Damn it! Damn it!" He glanced at the gas gauge. Three quarters. That would be enough for now. Unless she had plans to drive around the city all night. He had no idea. Maybe if she led him into parts of town where there was less traffic, he'd feel better about being in the stolen truck. Not so many cops. Less eyes to see what he had in mind.

SIXTEEN

Four hours into his concern. It was after nine, according to the watch on his wrist. Dark outside. Quiet house. No Natasha. Ryan left his third voicemail. No contact all day. His face wore frustration. Where the hell she was specifically, he had no idea. Where she was in general, that was a different story. Somewhere in town. That was all he'd let himself assume.

Coffee was lukewarm. He stared at the top of the desk. She'd been in his files. She wasn't trying to hide the fact. Santori's file was in the middle of his desk. He'd searched the computer's history. She'd looked up his address. Why? What would be the point? He wasn't going to go back to his house for a forgotten pair of socks or underwear. Even she would know that. Too iffy. Santori must know the place was being watched. She'd printed out a long list of Motels and Hotels. She was clever. He was staring at the same list. He'd printed it out from the computer's memory of recent documents.

Her cryptic note about being stressed. Needing to get away. Bunch of crap! She wasn't a runner. Nat was stand your ground. Deal with it. Deal with the consequences of dealing with it. It was one of the qualities he liked about her personality. She was strong. Could be feminine even sultry when she wanted. Played around the edges of vulnerable but could bite like a rabid, frothy-mouthed dog if needed.

He knew what she was up to. She was armed. In more ways than one. Armed with a list of motels and hotels in the area surrounding Santori's old digs. Armed with her .40 cal. The latter made him nervous. Swallowed a mouthful of coffee. Tasted old. Bitter. Made him shudder.

She was doing his job. Detecting. Tracking down the bad guys. Maybe out of her league. She was smart enough. Still a woman though. Already been grabbed and held once. Did she think this was some kind of video game? It was why the largest percentage of cops throughout the country, eighty at last count, were men.

He could task half dozen detectives. Get a few of the blues that were in cars on the streets, to shake down the motel and hotel managers. He made the call.

"Hey Cap'." Calling Captain Jules after hours wasn't S.O.P. unless it was "High protocol Police business". "It's Detective Ryan."

"I know who it is Detective." Jules was probably looking at the caller I.D. "I have caller I.D. I know your voice. That makes me two for two." He waited. "This important?"

"I'm thinking ya. It could turn into a situation." Ryan took a breath. Waited.

"Well get on with it Detective. Being two for two on knowing whose calling doesn't give me mind reading abilities. Where's this going?"

Ryan stifled a chuckle. Jules' mind was quick. He usually thought a couple steps ahead. "Well it seems Natasha has gotten a wild hair up and is out trying to track down the perp who abducted her."

"This the civilian you're living with? The one that put the finger on the seven eleven killer?"

"That would be her." He paused.

"What's she up to Detective?"

Another breath. "Well sir, it seems she's put together a list of Motels and Hotels in the immediate vicinity of the abductor's house. My guess is she's out there trying to find him."

Another pause.

"Isn't that something that we, as paid servants of the community, are supposed to be doing Detective?"

Ryan picks up a pencil and starts tapping the edge of the desk. "Yes sir and it is what we're doing. Not only is she duplicating what I already have our guys doing, we also have twenty-four-seven eyes on the perp's residence."

"So where did she get the idea of tracking him through local hotels and Motels?" Pause. "But more importantly, wouldn't she need and how did she get the perp's personal info Detective Ryan?"

Damn! That was a good question. "Well sir, uh, it seems she went through the case files that are on the desk in my office here at the house."

"Oh I see." The beginnings of condescension started creeping into his voice. "Do you think that's something, those files I'm talking about now, that should have maybe been, uhmm, maybe been kept a little more secured? You know, some kind of way to keep the general public, in this case the victim of a crime, from finding out personal information about the perpetrator. Information that could be used in a Court of Law to secure a conviction?"

The seat was getting hot. He felt pinned to it. "That's a fair, good and valid point sir." Breath. "It doesn't however change the reality of the situation. The situation she's put herself in I mean."

Pause on the line. He could feel the Captain's grip on the phone getting tighter. "Just what is the situation Detective? Why are you calling me at home this time of the night?"

"Calling for permission sir." Swallow. "I'd like to request a couple of men from the squad. Couple of guys to take this list I've put together and see if we can't track down her whereabouts. Maybe get a couple of units in the specific area to check a few of these Motels sir."

Longest pause so far. Ryan was about to ask if he was still there.

"Detective Ryan, if you weren't thought so highly of, not only by myself but by the Commissioner and the Mayor, I'd demote you for conduct detrimental. In your careless approach to safeguarding official police files, you have put in serious danger the victim of a previously committed felonious crime."

The pause was not so quiet. He could hear the Captain breathing. "You have also put in danger the alleged perpetrator of said crime." He stopped for a breath. "You can have one. One Detective from the squad. You have my permission to B.O.L.O. Miss Taylor's vehicle. Are we clear Detective?"

Ryan blew air. Didn't care if it was heard over the line. "Uh, yes sir. One Detective, myself and a B.O.L.O. on the car." He wanted to push for more. "How 'bout a couple of units in the general area of the perp's residence circulating a picture of the perp at a few Motels?"

"Well Detective if the B.O.L.O. finds the car, we'll find Miss Taylor. Not having her out there playing vigilante is my immediate concern. As it should be yours. Let's track her down and get her back where she's supposed to be. If she refuses to co-operate, well we always have protective custody now don't we."

This wasn't going as well as Ryan had hoped. Putting Natasha in protective custody, to keep her from tracking down the person who'd kidnapped and violated her, well that was going to royally piss her off.

"Detective Ryan. I'm waiting for you to respond. My wife is waiting. The peace and quiet of my evening at home are waiting."

"Yes sir. I understand completely sir."

"Good. Good. Now I suggest you get cracking. The hours are few when it comes to tracking down perps on the run. They tend to move around a lot. Here for minute. There for a minute. I won't ask how far behind you are. It must be substantial otherwise you wouldn't be calling for my help. Have a good night Detective. I'll expect a face to face report in my office at uh, let's say ten tomorrow morning?"

"Yes sir. Thank you sir. Good night sir."

He waited for the click on the line. Waited for the dial tone. Slammed the phone back in the cradle after hearing both. Fuck the point at which plastic shatters.

SEVENTEEN

Right hand held the wheel. Left hand flicked cigarette ashes out the half way down driver's window. Seventy mile an hour wind rushed by the open window. Headlights cutting through the shadowed night kicked back the dark blacktop as the Monte Carlo sped down the highway. Natasha's head shook gently from side to side, she was still chuckling in disbelief.

The second rate T.V. cop shows had been right on the money. Like Lazarus rising from the dead, the words written on the notepad had become visible. After shading the heavy indentations with the pencil edge, a possible clue to Lawnmower guy's destination had been revealed. She was determined to follow it. The trail would lead somewhere. Why write something down if it wasn't important? If you weren't oh maybe, possibly heading that way?

She would not be denied her justice. She was on a mission and drove like it. North Wenatchee Avenue took her onto old U.S. 97 on the west bank of the Columbia River. Not far from the U.S. 2 connector road. The interchange would carry her east across the river, then turn her north. From there it was a straight shot all the way up to Tonasket.

She'd make the left turn through town onto Fourth Street to pick up Loomis-Oroville Road on the west side of the Okanogan River. L-O Road would send her through the most picturesque areas of Washington's foothills. She'd be driving past a smattering of Finger Lakes and small rivers, coming into Nighthawk from the south. From the back side.

Nighthawk. The name triggered something somewhere in her brain. She worked her memory. "A small ghost town?" She mumbled. On the bank of the Similikeen River? She thought so. A border crossing town of sorts. She let those thoughts settle. Let them simmer. Opened her mind. Let the recollections slowly come.. Flicked the butt out the open window. Her mind drifted back. The years peeled away like the layers of an onion.

Then it hit her. When it did, it came all at once. Like being inundated under a waterfall. She almost drove off the highway. "Holy Christ!" She blurted out loud. Nighthawk was in timber and mining country. Their old cabin was in timber country. Palmer Lake. That's where the old cabin was. On the north shore. Or where it used to be.

Palmer Lake was off Loomis-Oroville Road west of Tonasket. "O.K. be calm." She told herself. Glance into the rearview mirror. Headlights. Maybe a half mile or so back. Flip up the turn signal. Lift off the gas. Spot the shoulder in the headlights. Loose gravel. Pull over slow and easy. Come to a stop. Shift the transmission into park. Breathe.

Grabbing her phone, she opened the map program. Washington State. How could she have missed it? So engrossed on the big picture directions to Nighthawk, she'd missed the obvious smaller details.

She held her breath. There was Tonasket. There was the turn-off onto Loomis-Oroville Road that would take her all the way to Nighthawk. Used her fingers to pinch open the map. The details got bigger. There was Palmer Lake. Open it larger again. She could see where the cabin should be. Not far from the Lake. Quarter to a half mile. "Survival mode requires you to have a

dependable source of clean water." Daryl's words echoing through her brain.

      *   *   *

"Whoa!" Albert blurted from about a half mile back. He watched her turn signal come on. Saw her car pull over to the side of the highway. He followed her lead. Spotted the shoulder. Eased over. Reached quickly for the headlight switch. Killed the lights. Now what the hell was she doing? Was she out of gas? He was just above a quarter tank. According to the last highway sign the next gas was twenty miles. He had more than enough. Maybe she had some other mechanical problem? Thinking. Thinking.

A maniacal leer grew, overcoming and slowly transforming his face. This was the perfect spot. No witnesses. Nobody around for miles. Quick glance in the rearview. Nothing. Dark as the back end of his subconscious. Like it had a mind of its own his hand slid down his leg, heading for his ankle. Heading for the sheath. If he was quiet, he would be on her before she knew it. Drag her from the car. Put a smile under chin from ear to ear.

     *   *   *

Natasha's eyes were riveted on the screen of her phone. She poured over the details. Her brain awash with memories the map's details dredged up. She worked on coming to grips with the fact that she'd be chasing down Lawnmower Guy in and around the same area she'd spent camping with her Dad all those years ago. A tight-lipped grin pulled at her lips. That would put the advantage in her favor.

     *   *   *

Albert pulled the shifter out of park. Dropped it easily down into drive. Kept his foot off the brake. He wanted no lights. Wanted no sound to alarm her. The truck idled along the shoulder. Closer. He was in full stealth mode. The sound of the tires crunching over the shoulder gravel seemed annoyingly loud. He crept forward. Less than fifty yards now.

     *   *   *

Natasha closed the phone. Her head fell back against the headrest. Eyes closed, a heavy sigh rushed through pursed lips. The Monte sat idling, headlights still on. The side of the road was empty. Slow head turn out the passenger window. Nothing. Darkness.

Surrounded by pitch black. "Get a grip." She muttered lighting another cigarette.

The Monte was low on gas. Less than a quarter. She remembered seeing a road sign for gas and food a couple of miles back. Twenty miles she thought it said. Her hand reached. Pulled the shifter into drive. Checked the driver's side mirror. Nothing. The Monte eased off the shoulder back onto the highway. She pushed the gas pedal. The back tires chirped coming from the gravel onto the blacktop jerking the car ahead. She had no idea how close she'd come. Close to not making it anywhere. Let alone to Nighthawk.

*   *   *

"Damn it!" Albert spat the words through snarled lips. He watched her car pull away from the shoulder picking up speed. His foot pressed down on the gas. The stolen truck lurched forward. The back tires churning up the shoulder gravel before they bit into the highway pavement. He knew his first chance at eliminating her had just evaporated. His face tightened, grim with determination. The next chance would have to be better. His eyes glued to the fading taillights in front of him. "I'll have your ass sooner or later." He muttered as he began closing the gap. "You can count on that."

*   *   *

She drove with a purpose. How far ahead of her Lawnmower man was didn't matter. She knew or was pretty sure of what he was up to. He'd get close enough to the Canadian border then make a run. He knew he was wanted. Kidnapping and Rape were serious crimes. Her advantage was that she didn't think he knew he was being followed.

Her tongue darted. Licking her lips unconsciously. She'd track him down. Make him pay for the humiliation. Her jaw tightened. She reached inside her purse. Bad day to quit smoking. Felt the butt of the gun. The thought of a round jacked in the chamber gave her a shot of courage. Pulling the smokes out, she lit one sucking the smoke down. Blew it hard at the windshield. She cruised through the interchange, the speedometer pushing seventy. Turned onto U.S. 2 north. Seventy crept up to seventy-five.

G.P.S. in her phone showed her the route to Nighthawk. Two, maybe two and a half hours. Maybe an hour and a half if she kept her foot in it. She set the cruise control at seventy-five. She'd stop at the next truck stop. Snacks and water, cigarettes for sure.

Her phone was showing multiple messages from Ryan. Damn it. She had to come up with a plan for Ryan. Guilt was not what she wanted to fertilize their growing seedling of a relationship. She knew he'd understand her reasons. She also knew he'd never agree with her methods or her solution. Then again, it wasn't his body that had been violated. He wasn't the one who'd had to endure the humiliation.

Too much time to get bored. Too much time to think on long drives. Headlights approached. Coming out of the pitch dark then flashing by. Stay focused she told herself. Stay on top of it. Maybe if she got Lawnmower guy tied to a chair in his underwear. Maybe he wouldn't be so tough. "Stop!" She heard her voice echo inside the car. There was already enough revenge fuel built up inside of her. She needed calm. She needed a clear head.

Out of control emotions only generated out of control actions. Sporty was right. Have a plan so tight it would give someone a migraine trying to figure it out. His words floated in. "You think all it takes is to put bullets in a paper target? Really? You think that, you're stupid." She wasn't stupid.

Her hand reached out for the radio. The lights lit. The soft-sided C.D. storage case next to her on the front seat held an eclectic mix. The player's mechanics clicked and hummed as it sucked in a C.D. Steely Dan. Aja. "Big Black Cow" fell out of the speakers.

* * *

Ryan's blood shot eyes looked back from the rearview mirror. He'd been running the brown undercover all night. They were both beat. Both needed fuel and sleep. Bone tired. He was pissed. Her unanswered cell. Everything went to voicemail. A B.O.L.O. had been issued on the Monte. Nothing had come back. Yet. There was no sign of her anywhere. She'd slipped into the ether.

He had Manny Salvatore, a ten year veteran Detective canvassing motels on the west side. Ryan was canvassing motels on the eastside. North and south were going to be next.

The fact that she wasn't answering her phone made him edgy. Made him tight in the gut. Was she ignoring him? Maybe she couldn't answer. In some kind of trouble. "Shit!" He barked out loud. Staring out the windshield his hand slapped the steering wheel. His eyes spotted the driveway.

He pulled into the "River View Suites". Parked in front of the office. Grabbing the manila folder with Santori's eight by ten, he slid out from behind the wheel. Stood with his hands on the roof above the door. Took a deep breath and started for the office.

"Manny 30 to Ryan 47."

Ryan stopped mid-stride. Jumped back to the driver's door. Yanked it open. Fell onto the seat. Grabbed the radio. What had Manny found? He hoped it wasn't a body. Her body. His voice gave tense. "Go for Ryan."

"Ya 47 I've hit the end of the Westside list over."

"Copy that 30."

"I'm gonna 10-19 the barn. Beat to crap. Pick it up tomorrow. Copy?"

"Ya. I know the feeling. I'm on the last one on the eastside list. Thanks for hangin' in dog. 'Preciate it."

"10-4. I'll see you at the sunrise. Something breaks, holler me."

"Ya 10-4. I'll do it. Go ahead. Pack it in. See you at the store in the morning. We'll hit 'em north and south."

"Copy that. Manny 30 Dispatch."

"Dispatch. Go 30."

"I'm 98 in the field. I'll be ears on, 10-19 your location."

"Copy 30. 10-19 my location."

Ryan swung the driver's door closed. He was disappointed. He was tired. He was hungry. He needed a break. Natasha had tenacity. She'd taken this on by herself. Shook his head slowly in admiration of her determination. He approached the motel office, manila folder in hand. Swinging the door open he spotted an older guy behind the counter. Looked sixtyish or so. Maybe fifty with a few hard years thrown in. It happens. Walking up he gave the old guy his concerned cop look.

The old guy stared back. He made Ryan for a cop as soon as the brown undercover pulled onto the lot.

"Hey." Ryan said approaching the counter.

The old man nodded. Waited. Knew there was more to come. Age does that. At least for most folks.

Ryan stood at the counter. Sucked in a breath. Opened the folder. Slid out Santori's picture. Spun it to face the old guy. Began the spiel.

"Seen this guy around?"

The old man stared at the photo. Looked up at Ryan's face. Held his eyes. Looked back down at the photo. "You related to this uh, fellow?"

Ryan spotted the name tag pinned to the old guys left shirt pocket. Felt his aggravation level rising. He bit the ends of the words off as they came out.

"Tell me Scott, do I need to be related to him to ask if you've seen him?"

"Cop huh?"

"Pull the badge if you want." Ryan replied. His eyelids arrowed. Gave the old man stern. Made a motion to reach around behind for his wallet.

"Nah. I made the car when you pulled in." He smiled a little when he said it. Ryan nodded. You didn't have to major in rocket science or brain surgery to pick out an undercover car. More antennas stuck to the roof and trunk lid than an alien spaceship. The blacked-out, no hub cap tires. Not to mention the spotlights on opposite corners of the windshield above the fenders.

"Got a key right here." He stated turning and reaching into the cubby hole between six and eight. Empty. His face got confused. "Well that's odd." He mumbled. "Have to talk to the day girl Trudy. She knows to put the keys back when she's done cleaning the rooms."

"You mean this guy was here?" Ryan's brain was starting to fire. Coming up to speed. He was tired but the old guy indicating Santori had been here sent a shot of adrenalin through his body. The tip and sides of his tongue were wet with it.

"Yep. He was here alright. Left this morning. Early. I can check the register. Tell you when he checked out." Scott made a move for the register. "We log all that stuff." He said with a sense of pride.

"What room?" Ryan shot at him. It stopped Scotty's move to the register.

"Well now that's what I just reached for. Key ain't there though."

"The master. You got one of those?" The tension in his voice was growing by the second.

Scott nodded. Pulled open a drawer below the counter. Handed Ryan a key attached to a thin three inch wide by six inch long piece of metal. "That'll get you in any door on the site."

"Great!" Ryan barked grabbing for the key and turning abruptly. "There'll be Crime Scene guys here in a bit to go through room seven." Ryan started for the office door.

"Well I suppose that's up to you. Won't find much though."

That stopped Ryan in his tracks. He turned to face Scott.

"Why's that?" Ryan asked.

"Day girl cleans before she leaves for the day. Room seven should be spic and span. Trudy's a good worker. Does her job well." Scott might have looked a little smug if Ryan had stayed to notice but the office door was already closing. He was jogging towards room seven.

EIGHTEEN

Just as the sign on the side of the road had stated, nineteen point five miles later the glow from the multiple overhead lights lit the area around the gas pumps and the parking lot like a revival for the second coming of Jesus Christ. Natasha pulled up to the pump closest to the Mini Mart front door and killed the engine. A quick glance in the rear view to check her face and hair and she was out the driver's door.

It was a ten pump Truck Stop. Two rows of four for gas and one double diesel pump sitting by itself. Not much business she thought scanning the parking lot on her way inside the Mini Mart. A couple of long haulers, one at the pump fueling up and one parked sorta by the exit idling. Maybe he was mapping his route. Maybe he was napping from driving twelve or fourteen hours. Whatever.

She pulled the single glass door open stepping into "Showtime." They must spend a ton on electricity she thought as the multiple rows of fluorescent overhead lights lit up the interior like Klieg lights at a Hollywood premier. Jesus Christ. She visibly squinted while making her way through aisles of snacks, cans of beans, band-aids, toilet paper and anything else a long hauler might think he'd need to make his destination.

She hit the coffee machine for a sixteen ounce French Roast. Abandoning her "dead calorie" rule she grabbed two or three four inch oatmeal cookies. Half a dozen spicy beef jerkys and four sixteen ounce bottles of water. She glanced around, just her and the counter kid. Hmmmm. Let's see if I can still do it. She thought walking up to the counter.

The kid was maybe seventeen or eighteen. Acne on his forehead like a sheet of eighth inch bubble wrap. Had the beginnings of moustache hair struggling to make a go of it but maybe it was gonna take another year or two.

"Howdy Ma'am." He gave her his best "I'm in charge" smile. "You see anything else you like?" He asked with a leery grin.

She had to bite the inside of her bottom lip to keep from laughing out loud. Hey at least he was man enough to cast the line. Too many boys his age were to squeamish to even hold the worm.

"Uh, nah, I just need forty bucks on pump, uh," she turned her head to check the number. "Uh, number two."

His name tag said Dennis and Dennis' face was getting a tad blushy. The realization that he was in ten miles over his head was sinking in.

"Right." He started. "Forty on number two and eight-fifty for the coffee and snacks. Anything else?" He realized he'd already gone down that road and his ears started to get a little crimson. She could see moisture was starting to gather on his bubble wrap forehead.

She dug out two twenties and a ten from her wallet.

He dropped his eyes to the pile of bills she'd dropped on the counter, grabbing for them with quivering fingers. Punching buttons on the cash register, he pulled her change out when the drawer popped open. He held it out towards her and she made a point of touching his skin on his hand as she took it. Just as she was stuffing the change in her wallet she remembered the cigarettes. "Oh uh Dennis can you grab me two packs of Marlie Lights. The long ones." She made a point of locking eyes with him when she said long.

His Adam's apple visibly rode the elevator up and down as he made every effort to swallow and maintain his cool. "Uh, ya, sure." Cool was gone. Driven away by the voice squeak. He tried clearing his throat before speaking again. A little less squeak but now there was a tremble. "Six-fifty." He vibratoed.

Another ten dollar bill his way and another three-fifty in change her way along with a another touch of skin on her part. She could see a tiny trail of sweat running down the side of his face. Poor boy she thought. "Thanks." She breathed at him. "Thanks for everything." She smiled, turned and let her hips propel her towards and out the door.

It was just a little fun, she told herself walking over to where she'd parked by the number two pump. She could see inside while she pumped her gas and Dennis was watching her like an Owl watched the night.

*   *   *

Down the highway a quarter mile away another pair of eyes watched. Watched her every move, for completely different reasons.

It might get a little complicated. It was surely going to test his patience but Albert had to wait. He had to time it so he was pulling in as she was leaving. He'd have to move fast. Get gas and whatever he was going to eat. Not letting her get too far out of sight. Use the same pump. Run in. Pay. Run out. Pump the gas. Shouldn't take too long. Then drive like Hell to catch up to her again. Anticipating the details was ratcheting up his anxiety to a level he wasn't used to. "Damn, damn, damn it." He muttered. His forehead broke with sweat.

*   *   *

She pulled away from the number two pump and parked before driving towards the Gas Station exit that would lead her back to the Highway. She glanced down at her snack variety, unceremoniously displayed on the passenger seat. She removed the plastic wrapper, bit a hunk off an Oatmeal cookie and slurped at her coffee. The French roast was hot enough to soften the Oatmeal cookie and the act of chewing and swallowing cleared some of the long drive dullness from her head.

Reaching over, she opened the map on her phone and concentrated on the display. She knew where she was and where she thought she needed to go. Had she not been so tunnel visioned on the map she might have noticed the truck pulling up to the pump furthest away from her.

*   *   *

Albert watched her pull over and stop. He watched her head drop and stare at something. He waited and then made the decision. Quietly easing open the driver's side door, he slunk silently out. He couldn't do it here he told himself. There was the clerk inside the store. A witness. Prob'ly one of those "do good sons-a bitches" who'd get his license plate and remember his description. No, he'd have to wait. The fuel tank on the truck however couldn't wait.

Taking furtive glances at her to make sure she wasn't aware, he stepped quickly through the front door of the store. His face took its usual nondescript facade. Eyes down, he made his way through the snack aisle grabbing a few chocolate bars, hit the coffee bar for a cup of black and then the counter.

"Hey." The counter man mumbled. He wasn't sure how bad of a character this guy was but his neck hairs were standing at attention. "That be it for you?" He asked.

"Naw." Albert leaked the words out his closed mouthed lips. "I need ten bucks on number 9." He nodded towards the gas pumps making sure that the object of his affection was still where he'd last seen her.

"Right. That'll be $14.75." The kid behind the counter stated. He took the twenty dollar bill Albert offered and turned to the cash register.

Albert had always been fast with his hands. He could've been a card shark magician with his sleight of hand skills. He chose a different path in life as we have come to find out. So after giving the kid behind the counter a twenty dollar bill, he slipped his hand inside his pants pocket, slipped out the 7-11 murder knife and plunged it into the kid's stomach when he turned back from the cash register to hand Albert his change.

Before he had a chance to close the till, the kid's legs buckled and he sank to the floor like a sack of flour. Albert spied the open till before the kid's body had settled into a clump of dying flesh and was quick to reach out and relieve the cash register of a handful of bills. You can take the thief out of the city but you can't take the thief out of the thief. Another check on the woman and his heart jumped. The car was gone.

Albert bolted through the store's front doors on the run. He stared down the highway and barely spotted two fading red taillights in the distance. He couldn't wait get gas. He never paid for it anyway. Not that that made any difference.

Jumping in behind the wheel Albert fired up the engine, dropped it into gear and left the gas stop in a hail of smoke and squealing tires. With his foot smashing the gas pedal firmly into the floorboard, the engine was soon whining at eighty-five miles an hour.

It took about ten minutes but he was soon within an eighth mile of her taillights and closing. No more kid gloves with this bitch. It was time to go on the offensive.

*   *   *

Natasha flicked the last of her smoke out the driver's side window and quickly powered it up. The night air blowing in was a tad chilly. She glanced in the rear view mirror at the headlights coming up from behind and wondered who else would be heading her direction at this time of night.

NINETEEN

Ryan jabbed the master key into the lock while simultaneously shoving the door open. His nose told him the manager had been correct. The room smelled of disinfectant and it looked like it had been recently buttoned up. The bedspread was wrinkle free and flat, the pillows plumped and tucked underneath.

The trash can in front of the nightstand beside the bed held a fresh empty plastic bag insert. Trudy hadn't missed anything he mused while leaving the bathroom. There was a new paper wrapped drinking glass sitting on the side of the sink, the shower curtain was pulled back exposing a clean tub with fresh towels hanging from the towel rack.

He walked back into the main room, his head on a swivel. The trash can in the kitchen was also newly plastic bag inserted. There was nothing here. He could feel it. There was no life in the room other than the one he'd brought in with him. He was here for a reason though, he knew that. He headed back to the door, his head still chewing on something.

"Here's your key back." He tossed the key on the counter between them.

"Didn't find anything huh?" The manager said with just a tad of smugness "I said Trudy did a good job." He added puffing his chest a little.

Ryan held his tongue. His eyes swirling the area behind the counter. He noticed a fresh bag in the trash can in the corner and had a thought.

"You had a lot of roomers the past twenty-four?" He asked. A thought had landed in his swirling brain.

"A couple." The manager replied suspiciously. "You wanna see those rooms too?"

"Nope but I do want to see where your roomers made any phone calls." Ryan was chasing a thread. "You got a copy of outgoing phone calls?"

"Ya, I suppose I can let you have a look." Scott replied. He reached under the counter and handed over a hard cover ledger. "Here you go. That'd be for room seven, five, three and eleven."

Ryan opened the book on the counter and wrote down the four numbers generated by the phone in room seven. "Great. Thanks for your help Scott. 'ppreciate it."

Ryan turned before Scott could reply and headed out the door while pulling his phone. He dialed the first number. It was for a local food delivery and he quickly hung up. The second number just rang no answer, no machine. He punched in the third number and got an answer. "Loomis Breeze B and B. How can help you?"

Ryan was stumped. What the hell was Nighthawk? "Where am I calling?"

"'Scuse me? This is the Loomis Breeze Bed and Breakfast establishment. We have daily, weekly and monthly rates. We can provide a continental breakfast and dinner service is available. Now how can I help you?"

"Well I guess you can help me by telling me where you are?"

"We're in the northern part of the state a few miles from the Canadian border crossing of Nighthawk, Washington and Chopaka, Canada." Came the reply.

Ryan's brain started adding. Lawnmower man was making a break. Why the Hell he had chosen Nighthawk didn't matter but Ryan now had a hunch burning his belly. "Great thanks for your time." He quickly disconnected and dialed Captain Jules.

"Ya. Who's this?" Jules barked. "You know what time it is?"

"Hey Cap' it's me Ryan. I think I have my finger on what's going on."

There was a pause and Ryan could hear breathing through the earpiece. "You still have a job Ryan? Where the Hell are you and what are you doing?

"Well sir as far as I know you're still my Boss and I've got a lead I'm gonna follow, that'll take me out of town for a day or two. With your permission of course."

More dead air and breathing. "You think you know how to resolve this mess with this woman and not turn up any dead bodies Detective?"

"I think that may be the case sir. I think I have a reliable bit of information that will get us back the bail jumper and the woman chasing him. Without too much muss or fuss."

Again with the dead air and breathing. "Well then go ahead Detective but do me a favor. Keep me in the loop, keep it clean, you know. No runs, no drips, no errors. Can you do that?"

Ryan held back a chuckle. "Yes sir I believe I can keep the damage to none or minimal."

"Well I'd prefer none of course. Goodnight." There was a dial tone.

Heading out the Motel office door, Ryan opened the map of Washington app on his phone and Found Nighthawk. He quickly picked out a route and slid behind the wheel. The undercover shot out of the parking lot amid the protest of rubber on pavement and Ryan was third in line on the way towards the Washington/Canadian border town of Nighthawk.

*   *   *

Albert watched the glow of the red tail lights getting closer. Switching off his headlights he used their location to keep him centered on the highway behind her car. The fifty yard distance soon became twenty. Albert pushed the gas pedal further down. Twenty yards turned to ten, then five. He could easily see her silhouette in the driver's seat through the rear window. The game was about to go to a whole new level. The front bumper of the truck made contact with the rear bumper of her car.

    *   *   *

  The thump from behind was hard enough to jolt her head back. A shot of adrenalin shot through her body prickling the hair on her arms and neck and tingling the sides of her tongue. "What the Hell!" She blurted, staring into the rear view mirror.
  She could barely pick out the grill of a pickup truck just as she felt another jolt from behind. She could feel her heart beat quickening as her grip on the steering wheel tightened. The last jolt had sent the back end of the Monte jumping a little sideways on the blacktop. She had to jerk and grip the wheel to keep the car going straight. Her forearm muscles bristled.

    *   *   *

  Albert grinned crazily. His eyes were wide. The adrenalin was flowing just like it did when he knifed the woman behind the counter and the kid back at the gas station. He watched as the back end of her car jumped from side to side. "Ha ha ha!" He bellowed. "I got you now bitch! It won't be long 'fore your time on this planet will come to an end!"
  He gunned the gas and knocked her rear bumper again. This time the back end of her car went from parallel to the white line to sliding sideways. He could see her fighting the wheel through her rear window. He laughed out loud again.

    *   *   *

  Natasha was in a panic. She was a N.A.S.C.A.R. fan but had no idea how they did what they did. She jerked the steering wheel from side to side trying her best to keep her car on the blacktop and off the gravel shoulder. She knew as soon as her front wheels hit the gravel, the chances of her keeping the car on the pavement decreased dramatically. The next thought that came waterfalling through her mind was who the Hell was behind her and why were they doing this?

It was too dark to see anything in the mirror, other than truck grill. Another big bump and she felt the back end of the Monte jerk hard to the right. She heard rubber squealing on hard blacktop. Jerking the wheel to the right then left straightened her out some but the front of her car headed into the oncoming lane. Her jaw clenched so fast she about bit her tongue. Then she had a thought.

Natasha veered into the oncoming lane and punched the brake. She watched the pickup truck start to pass the passenger side of the Monte. She quickly jerked the wheel to the right just as the left quarter panel of the pickup lined up with her right front fender.

* * *

Albert gave her one more forceful punch on her back bumper and watched the rear of her car start sliding to the right. She was losing it. Then she caught it but suddenly slowed and he started to pass her. He was almost by her when she turned into him, catching the truck's left quarter panel.

* * *

There was more squealing rubber. The front of the truck shot across the highway and the front end of the Monte spun right on the soft gravel shoulder.

Out of the corner of her eye she saw the pickup tip to the right and then it was on its side sliding down the highway. The Monte's front tires slid through the gravel as she jammed the brake pedal.

She watched the side of the road coming at her and then she was off the road and into a three foot ditch. Hard stop into the bank of the ditch. Her chest thrust into the steering wheel knocking the air out of her. She gasped for a breath. Big or small, she didn't care. Any breath at all.

* * *

Albert's back tires screamed on the blacktop and he saw the horizon shifting away from level. With a resounding crash the pickup was passenger side down on the pavement. He found himself lying up against the passenger door, his face a few scant inches from the grating blacktop. He heard a yelp from somewhere and a shot of pain from his right shoulder that ran down his arm.

What the Hell had happened? He was in control behind her knocking her off the highway and now he was the one knocked over. He smelled gas and knew that was not a good thing.

"Have to get out." His brain was shouting messages at him. The truck had come to a grinding halt. Had to get out. He had to fight gravity. He reached for the steering wheel with his left hand and pulled himself as upright as he could. Switched his left to his right hand and there was the blinding pain.

     *   *   *

Her headlights glared into the ground. Not a sight she was used to. Reached for the door handle and with a groan the driver's side door swung open. She spotted the pickup lying on its side ten or fifteen yards down the highway. She stood at the side of the Monte trying to clear her head and recover her wits.

She reached down beside the driver's seat and pulled on the trunk release handle. The trunk slowly yawned open as she staggered to the back and her duffle with the survival gear she'd packed.

     *   *   *

Gritting his teeth he reached for the window control. He had to wind it around with his left hand to lower the window so he could climb out. His right hand had to hold the steering wheel while he cranked. He almost cried out with the pain generating from his right shoulder.

     *   *   *

Natasha stood on the shoulder of the road. Get your bearings she reminded herself. She saw far enough into the darkness to see trees. Looked like on both sides of the highway.

She was standing on the side of the road that ran through some kind of foresty woods. The Monte was pointed into the side of a three foot deep ditch. It was going nowhere. She didn't have time to wait for triple "A". She had to hold back a laugh at the absurdity of the thought.

She mentally went over the contents of the duffle hanging from her right hand. There was a compass, a map of Nighthawk, a penlight, a canteen full of water, a bottle of Excedrin, some first aid items. Most important was her Glock, the silencer and six fifteen round magazines.

She glanced over at the pickup and saw a round anomaly sticking up through the driver's side window opening. A head! It was a head! The head of the person who had caused this horrific piece of shit.

As pissed off as she was, she was tempted to pull the Glock out and pop around into the head of whomever it was that was trying to crawl out of the wreck.

   *   *   *

Just tall enough. Albert was tall enough to stand against the inside of passenger door and stick his head out the driver's side window into the cool night air. His eyes had to adjust to the darkness. The truck's headlights pointed off the side of the road into the leading edge of a growth of trees some fifteen yards away.

Turning his head he could see down the highway they'd been travelling. There was a road sign twenty or so yards away. Barely readable in the darkness, it stated Nighthawk was five miles down the road. It meant nothing to him. It would however when she saw it, mean a great deal to Natasha.

He pushed up with his legs trying to limber himself out the window. There was nothing for support. Nothing to grab onto. The ground was four feet away and he lurched himself out the window, freefalling onto the highway's gravel shoulder. Catching his left foot on the steering wheel, twisted and spun him upside down onto the ground. This time he did holler. "Ow, ow, ow! God damn it!" He spat. He hobbled himself into a sitting position staring at the bottom chassis of the pickup. He still smelled gas. Gotta move he told himself. Gotta move.

    *   *   *

She watched in disbelief as the lanky body extricated itself out the driver's side window. It looked vaguely familiar. Creepy familiar. She caught the profile in the abstract headlight and the disbelief turned to fear. It was him! It was the guy she'd pointed out to Ryan. Selma's killer! Flight or fight took over her brain. She gripped the strap of the duffle and took off running.

  She spotted the sign after putting ten yards or so between her and the wreck. The familiarity of it all started to sink in. She was on the highway into Nighthawk and as best as she could tell, about three miles from their old cabin. There was a dirt road cut-off a mile or so down this highway that dead-ended a quarter mile off the highway. It was then about a two mile hike to their old cabin. She wondered if it was still standing.

    *   *   *

He heard the footsteps on the highway as he rose up from the side of the highway. They were running footsteps. His left ankle bit when he put weight on it causing him to shift his weight to the right. He stared in the direction of the retreating footsteps. "Damn it!" He spat. She's getting away.

He reached down to the side of his left boot. felt the handle of his blade and pulled it out. Started his limping walk after the fading footsteps. They were running but Albert didn't care. He was resilient. He'd spent time in jail. He knew how to get through bad shit. He'd done it his whole life. Fact is his whole life had been full of bad shit. So he limped on . . . . as best he could.

*   *   *

Ryan held the speedometer at ninety. The fence posts along the side of the road went by in a blur. The palms of his hands were moist in their grip of the steering wheel. He had no idea how far ahead they were. All he knew was that he wasn't there. He hoped for the best but that didn't loosen the tightness that gripped his gut. The undercover was eating up the highway, just not as fast as Ryan wanted. He knew he couldn't beat the car to death. That wouldn't do either him or her any good. He had to keep it running. Keep the abuse to a minimum.

It was another hour of gripping the wheel and staring his bloodshot eyes into the darkness before he spotted the headlights at an off angle to the highway. He lifted his aching foot off the accelerator, giving his calf muscles a chance to relax. He coasted up to the scene his foot pulsing on and off the brake pedal.

Her car was nose first into a three foot deep ditch. Driver's side door agape and the trunk lid yawning open. No sign of anyone. No sign of life. He stepped down to peer into the front seat. Nothing. Back seat was the same. The yawning trunk held a spare and some road flares. The jack and tire iron were askew along with a pair of women's cowboy boots.

He turned to the other vehicle. A pickup of some kind lying on its side headlights shining into the side of the road and into the woods beyond. He walked back to his undercover and pulled his duty flashlight out from under the driver's seat. The bright light illuminated the scene. There were black tire marks scrawled across the blacktop and deep pitted scrapes where the pickup had slid fifteen yards or so down the road.

Walking to the front of the truck he shone the light into the cab. Empty. Heavy smell of gas and rubber permeated the area. Shining the light around the scene he saw footsteps in the side of the road gravel leading away from the truck in the same direction he'd been travelling. No Natasha and no pickup truck driver. He guessed there was a connection. A connection that probably wasn't good for Natasha.

*   *   *

Ten minutes into her jog Natasha came to the dirt side road. She stared into the darkness that enveloped her. Looking back down the highway she could see a faint glow from the trucks headlights but nothing else. She had no idea as to the health of the killer chasing her or if he even was. She felt confident that her time jogging had put some distance between them.

She felt safe enough to stop, catch her breath and come up with a plan. Reaching for the zipper of the duffle she opened the bag. Her hand gripped the Glock. Next was one of the fifteen round mags. She slapped it into the butt of the gun and jacked a round.

She slipped the Glock into the front of her waistband. There would be no need for the silencer. There was nothing discreet about what was about to go down. Pulling out the canteen she took couple of gulps and started feeling somewhat revived.

Digging around she pulled out the penlight, the compass and the map of Nighthawk. Lining up the compass with the map she was able to figure what direction their old cabin was and the town of Nighthawk itself.

She calculated distances and guessed she could be at their old cabin within an hour and Nighthawk itself in about ninety minutes. She zipped the bag, resolute in her goal to find Lawnmower man and end his time on the planet for violating her personal peace and space.

* * *

The going was slow but Albert was determined. He didn't after all have a choice. If the woman testified against him his life on the streets would cease to exist. His left ankle was making itself known for all the wrong reasons. His right shoulder had been throbbing the whole time. It throbbed less if he jammed his hand into his pocket to kind of support the joint.

He couldn't hear her footsteps on the highway any more but he knew she was up ahead. She had to be. Anyway there were only trees and forest on either side of the highway and he didn't figure she would've taken off into the woods.

He eventually came to the dirt side road. She was obviously long gone and he had no idea if she had kept going straight down the highway or made the right turn onto the dirt road. He stood there sniffing the air like a bloodhound on the trail of an escaped convict. What did his senses tell him? He closed his eyes and became one with the air. Feeling it for any movement. He had a sense, turned off the highway and started down the dirt side road.

* * *

Emilio Santori. A.K.A. the Lawnmower Guy had been walking for a while. Quite a while truth be told. There was no bus service to Nighthawk the ticket agent had been clear. Nighthawk was a ghost town. The close by border town of Chopaka wasn't a ghost town but the bus line didn't go to Canadian cities. Loomis was as close as the bus would take him.

He'd also been clear on the price of the ticket and that Loomis was just a hop, step and a jump to Nighthawk and the border crossing town of Chopaka Canada. Well a hop, step and a jump ended up being a little over ten miles and Emilio was bone tired.

His eyes had gotten used to the darkness and though barely visible as he broke through the trees, there were the ghostly frames of a building or two. The remnants of Nighthawk. He spotted a wedge shaped building and made his way to what he thought was the front entrance. The wood door had faded and was a heartbeat from giving in to the pull of gravity.

The two by four frame grudgingly held the graying one by four boards that gave it it's shape. The barely upright door groaned in protest as he pushed it open. He was looking for some place off the ground where he could stretch out and rest a bit before heading for the border town of Chopaka.

Rummaging around behind a closet door he found a couple of old army blankets that when the dust was shaken off, would do good enough to keep the night air from settling on top of him. A bench along the far wall was long enough and he settled down before the next round of hiking. The border and the freedom he hoped for was close enough to smell.

TWENTY

Natasha's infrequent use of her penlight kept the battery alive but also kept her from stumbling over broken branches that littered the forest floor. She was half an hour into her journey when she spotted the shape of the old cabin looming through the darkness in the trees. She was unprepared for the flood of feelings that washed over her stopping her in her tracks. The sharp catch of air in her throat gave way to relief that she'd finally made it.

The front door hung at a weird angle awkwardly from the top hinge and she opened it marginally to keep it from falling as she passed inside. She heard a rustling sound of claws skittering across the wooden floor and gave a yelp as it rushed passed brushing her leg on its way out the door. She reached for the Glock but held back on the trigger not knowing who might hear the shot echoing around the cabin.

Using the penlight, she spotted the kitchen table and it's four wooden chairs. Familiarity of the place slowly began to settle in. She grabbed a kitchen towel off the counter, shook it and then dusted off the seat of a chair facing the door. She dropped into it taking a load off her weary legs. Laying the Glock on the table she dusted off a spot in front of her then folded the towel for a pillow and rested her head beside the Glock. She let her right hand fall onto the Glock, quickly accessible if needed. She just wanted to close her eyes for a minute . . . .

*   *   *

Ryan crept the undercover along at just above idle speed. He was looking for a sign. Anything that would give him a clue. In short he came across the gravel side road off the main highway. His brain raced. If he had to guess, he guessed that the gravel road meant something. He wheeled the undercover onto it and ran it to its eighth of a mile end.

Killing the engine he got out sweeping his duty flashlight in a hundred and eighty degree arc across the end of the road where it illuminated the beginning of the tree line. There were a couple of disturbed areas directly in front of where he'd stopped the undercover. He guessed that that was as good a sign as he was going to get.

Popping the trunk he dug out two extra fifteen round mags and two sixteen ounce bottles of water. He opened a small carry-on bag and tossed the water, the mags and a couple of road flares in before zipping it closed. Closing the trunk he headed into the trees.

Keeping a good pace while trying not to stumble over fallen branches and other forest floor debris, in about fifteen minutes he'd worked up a good sweat He was able to spot disturbances in the underbrush to keep him moving in what he assumed was the right direction. He hoped his timing would be good enough to prevent Natasha from getting herself into more trouble than what she could deal with.

* * *

Albert was dead tired. His ankle was sore enough to keep him limping but not sore enough to stop his progress. His right shoulder had stopped throbbing but he kept his hand in his pocket just in case. He trod through the forest with one thought in mind.

He had to eliminate the woman. She was a threat to his freedom and he wasn't about to go back to three squares, a cot behind locked bars and a questionable roommate. So he kept on tramping through the damp forest undergrowth hoping he was on the right track.

He knew he was headed in the right direction after spotting it once and then a second and third time. Albert was sure that it wasn't a natural occurrence. A very small pinpoint of light revealed itself up ahead in the shadowy darkness in the trees. It moved jerkingly for few seconds then went out for a minute or two, then reemerged in a different location. A leering smile of satisfaction unfolded on Albert's exhausted face. The woman. It had to be. Nobody else would be out here in the middle of nowhere. He honed in on it and moved towards it.

The closer he got to the reoccurring light the quieter he tried to be. He was about fifty yards away when it went out and never came back on. He pointed his nose at where he last saw it and stealthed his way forward. Within five minutes he broke through the trees into a small clearing and spotted the cabin.

He stood quietly breathing the air. What could he feel? What was the universe telling him? His breathing slowed. He went to stalking mode. He focused his eyes and stared hard at the cock-eyed cabin door. Was she inside. waiting. Albert's palms got damp. He didn't like being at a disadvantage. Not knowing what was on the other side of the broken cabin door put him off. Made him swallow hard.

He slunk a step quietly forward. How could he turn the disadvantage in his favor? He was there now. The off kilter cabin door a foot in front of him. Should he trust that he could slither his way in without the door falling from its remaining hinge? God knows what kind of clamorous racket that would create.

Maybe he should just burst in Hell bent in surprising her and throwing her completely off guard? He, being the slinky, slippery fellow he thought he was, opted for the stealthy approach. He was after all a world class sneak who prided himself in his ability to move with stealth when necessary.

Albert's left hand reached slowly out until it came in contact with the worn wooden door. He gave it a gentle push and it moved. He pushed it more, moving it open an inch at a time. He was at a point where he was almost able to slink his way through the opening when the top hinge finally gave up. He could feel the door teeter inward and start to swing away from him. He unconsciously gasped. His right hand jabbed at the door handle but he missed and ended up pushing the teetering door with enough force to have it go crashing into the room. Had he had a plan to make a tumultuous shock and awe entrance this would have been perfect. Instead he was in shock and awe over how badly his plan had gone.

     *   *   *

Natasha was startled fully awake by the front door crashing into the room. Her right hand gripped the Glock and instinctively pointed it in the direction of the commotion. She spotted a large human shape and let go a double tap.

The clap of gunfire echoed around the wooden walled cabin causing her ears to immediately start ringing. The human shape dropped to the cabin floor shouting "what the Hell?" and "God damn it!" She didn't recognize the voice but knew she'd made a good choice about letting a couple of rounds go.

Reaching for the edge of the table, she flipped it forward onto its side, crouching behind Glock in hand, ready to let go another volley if needed. "Who's there!" She yelled out. There was no reply. "I'll shoot again!" She warned. Still no answer.

     *   *   *

Albert knew he was hit. Same shoulder that took a beating when the truck flipped over. Now it felt like it was on fire, hurt like Hell. He could see the overturned table and started to slither his way towards the edge closest to him. He heard her call out but he had no intention of answering and giving his location away. Knife in hand, he scraped around the edge of the table and spotted the crouching woman. Almost close enough he thought, another foot and she'd be in arm's length.

     *   *   *

Natasha's heart was beating like she'd never felt it before. She could feel it in every pulsing artery in her body. Her ears, the Carotids in her neck and her wrists were all thumping to the beat. She knew whoever it was, was down, she just didn't know where. High ground was the advantage in battle so she stood. Looked to the floor on her right and spotted a dark shape at the edge of the overturned table. "Hey you!" She barked. "Stop moving or I'll shoot!"

*   *   *

He figured now! He was close enough. He'd at least get her leg, drop her to the ground and then make a grab for the gun. He took a deep breath and lunged like an alligator coming out of the water after a gazelle that had wandered too close to the water's edge.

Her gun went off with a loudness that echoed off the old wooden walls. He never saw whether or not the knife made contact with her leg. Two of the four rounds she fired hit him in the back of his neck at about C-1 and C-2. The other two rounds hit the shoulder of the arm swinging the knife and it clattered harmlessly onto the floor.

Albert Tooms would not have to go back to the small cement walled room with the barred front door and an undetermined roommate. He would not have to go back anywhere. He would however go to the County Morgue and a city sponsored plot in the County Graveyard.

Nat's shaky hand slid the Glock back into her waistband. The barrel warm against her skin. She worked on slowing her breathing and calming her pulsating heart. Her eyes picked out an old wooden chair in the darkness. She sat staring down at the man who she now recognized as Selma's killer. Serves him right she thought. He was scum. Preyer of and on the weak and vulnerable. He was in the same category as Lawnmower Man. That thought triggered her into action.

She wasn't that far from Nighthawk and the dark night was to her advantage. Slipping her phone from her pocket it told her it was just going on two-fifteen. She had to get going if she wanted to keep the dark night in her favor. Deciding what to do with the dead man in the cabin was not a priority right now. Her next conversation with Ryan would sort out an answer to that.

She strode for the opening where the front door used to hang and into the dark night.

TWENTY ONE

Lawnmower man wasn't getting much rest. The sounds of the night and his fear of getting caught kept his eyes from staying closed for any length of time. The woolen army blankets he'd covered himself with kept most of the cold air in check but bouts of involuntary shivers kept his teeth chattering.

He kept on hearing things. Unknown and unanswerable sounds that as a city boy, were unfamiliar to his ears. He figured it was too early to head to the border crossing but he wasn't sure what the Hell their hours were. Did they open at eight or seven or even six in the morning? He didn't want to get there too early and have to answer a lot of questions.

Maybe he didn't have to cross at Chopaka at all. He could probably just wander through the woods until he was sure he was into Canada the just walk into the town like he lived there. A slow smile broke his face. That was a much better plan. No questions no halting answers. It was decided. A no muss no fuss crossing was the way to go.

    *   *   *

Natasha entered the ghost town at right around two thirty. The dilapidated buildings wore crowns of misery and disrepair. She couldn't see any life anywhere and she wondered if in fact Lawnmower Man was even here. She'd have to search each building one at a time. Slowly and carefully.

She remembered how big and strong he'd been while manhandling her into that chair and tying her up. His advantage had been the chloroform he used to subdue her. The smell of it triggered a memory in her brain.

She stepped passed a one storey house that the roof had collapsed inward and wrote it off as uninhabitable. She scuffled along through the dirt and gravel street towards a building that had a wooden sidewalk across the front and an upper floor with a balcony. It looked promising as the roof was still up offering some kind of protection from the elements.

She approached the wooden deck and stealthily stepped across the creaky boards to the entrance. Her penlight swept the interior of the ground floor revealing decades of neglect and decay. Across the main room were a set of stairs leading to the upper level. She thought about taking them up but the sweeping penlight revealed that only the first two thirds were still in place. The top section had given way and was nothing more than a pile of rubble littering the floor.

She stole her way around the main floor, poking her head and the penlight into three of what looked like four rooms. They were all dusty and abandon. As she approached the last room she heard a rustling sound that had her right hand whipping the Glock out of her waistband. She held it gut high and moved forward.

Was this room where Lawnmower Man had made his bed? She turned the light off and stepped as quietly as she could towards the open door. More rustling sounds. Sliding her finger from the gun frame to the trigger, she swung her body into the opening and hit the switch on the penlight. Empty!

While she stood there a slight breeze blew a scraggly branch against the wooden window frame. She would've chuckled if she hadn't been so scared.

She retraced her entry and stood in the doorway entrance. Another building across the street. Thinking about where she had to go and sucking in a deep breath, she stepped out into the street, nose pointed straight ahead.

*   *   *

At this point Emilio had given up on sleep. He huddled on the bench in a sitting position, wrapping the army blankets around his shoulders to stave off the night air. More sounds again. Scraping. Was it the sound someone would make while walking? He wasn't sure but was uncontrollably on edge. He couldn't just sit there shivering and play the wait and see game.

Tossing off the army blankets he jerked his head around the room looking for a quick way out besides the front door. He hurried towards a back door and rattled the handle. The building had obviously settled over the years throwing the frame out of square wedging the door tight against the frame.

*   *   *

Crossing the street, Natasha's senses ramped up. Something was going on that her instincts had picked up on. Gun drawn, she pointed it straight ahead waist high resting her hand on her hip bone. Something felt off about this building. She approached the front entrance warily. Her nostrils flared sucking all the available oxygen out of the air to feed her lungs and beating heart. She stepped through the entrance into the main room.

*   *   *

Lawnmower Man's breath caught in the back of his throat. He squeezed himself against the wedged door hoping he could overcome the world of matter and have the door absorb him through it into a different space and time. He could see the silhouette framed in the doorway outlined by the moon and stars. It looked smallish. He didn't think it was a man but why would a woman be out here in the middle of the night? Surely he could handle a woman without much help.

He took a step forward out of the shadows. "Hey you!" He shouted. "Get outta here!" He yelled in his best bravado voice.

The woman whirled in his direction and a shot rang out. The bullet missed and Emilio heard it slam into the wood beside his left arm. Splinters flew and Emilio dropped to the wooden floor. His breath was now coming hard and fast. Holy shit he thought. Who the Hell was she and why was she shooting at him?

"Hey Lawnmower Man." She spat in his direction. "Looks like I found you huh? You might remember me." She added. "If you think hard."

He unconsciously shook his head. He had no idea who she was even though her voice had a familiar sound to it.

"Looks like the roles are reversed now." She spoke quietly while pulling the penlight out of her pocket with her free hand and shining it in the direction of her fired shot. There he was, down on the floor, huddled against a door looking like a trapped animal. Fear had sucked any sign of life out of his face. She turned the penlight from him to her face.

"Recognize me now asshole?" She asked biting off the ends of the words. "Let's see if we can find a chair for you." She swept the light from left to right quickly taking inventory of the room's contents. She jerked the light back to Emilio. "Move and this situation will end quickly." She stated. "Quickly however is not what I'm looking for."

She kicked a hard-backed wooden chair in his direction. He jumped at the noise it made as it bounced across the floor shot in his direction.

"Have a seat my friend." She began. "I've been waiting a long time for this moment."

He realized who she was when the light splashed across her face for those few brief seconds. He knew he was in the middle of a bad situation and that broke a sweat over the whole of his body.

"You don't need to do anything that's gonna get you in trouble now." He tried to bargain. "We've both made mistakes in our life and I certainly beg for God's forgiveness for the mistakes that I've made and to those who I've done wrong."

Picking the chair up off the floor he stood it up on its four legs and stood behind it with the seat facing her.

"Well asshole if God was here," she replied, "he might be of a mind to forgive and forget. But as best as I can tell there's only you and me and I'm not big on forgetting and right now I'm not feeling very forgiving so have a seat." She barked the words through clenched teeth while jerking the light from him to the chair. She took three or four steps into the room putting him less than ten feet in front of her. She had to be wary. She'd dealt with his strength before and a cornered animal is the most dangerous kind.

Emilio followed her orders and sat up square in the chair, hands in his lap, staring straight ahead.

"Now if I had a mind, I'd have you naked and tied up." She began but I have no desire to get that close to you to tie you up. So I'll go for the other half. Stand up and take your clothes off." She gave the command with a wry smile pulling at the corners of her lips.

"What?" He said in disbelief.

"You heard me son of a bitch! Stand up and take your fucking clothes off!" This time she spat the directive at him with flecks of spit accompanying the words.

"Now wait a second . . . " was all he got our before the first shot rang out digging into the floor a foot from the front of the chair. Emilio yelped in surprise quickly jumping to his feet. "You don't need to . . . "

"You're wrong God damn it! I do need to!" She cut him off. "This is tit for tat jerk-off. You had me naked in a chair and that's how I'm going to have you. Now!" She put another round a foot or so closer to him.

Emilio's hands were visibly shaking as he reached for the buttons on his shirt. He began to haltingly undo them and within a minute or two slipped the shirt off and tossed it aside. There was no way to tell if he was quivering from fear or the cool air that was now washing over him. He stood and gave her a sorrowfully pleading look with his eyes.

"Sorry dirt bag you'll get as much sympathy from me as I got from you. Now carry on. Pants, shoes and everything in between." She was getting tired of standing and tired of holding the gun on him. Ya it was a smallish hand gun but it had some weight and she'd been holding it at gunpoint for a while now.

He dropped his hands to his waist and started fidgeting with his belt. It was taking too long so another shot rang out causing him to jump straight up six inches off the floor. "I'm doing it." He blurted. "I'm doing it!"

"Well hurry up damn it. You're taking too long." She shot back. "The end result is gonna be the end result but you're gonna damn sure do it my way!"

Emilio slipped his shoes off while standing and dropped the waist of his pants down around his ankles. He sat down in the chair as he pulled the legs off and tossed the pants aside. He was now only in his socks and underwear. "That's it." He stated defiantly. "I'm not doing any more."

Without hesitation Natasha let a round go that caught Emilio in the left shoulder spinning him through the chair to the floor. The .40 cal. Glock packed quite a wallop. It was why she bought it.

Emilio screamed in pain and gripped his left shoulder with his right hand. "Holy God! He hollered. "Stop this madness!"

"Madness?" She questioned. "You think this is madness? We haven't even started yet." She answered with a loud bark. "It was madness what you did to me. Remember? Now underwear off and back in the chair." She ordered.

Emilio was slobbering and groveled his way back to the chair. He ran through his options hoping to find a way out of his predicament.

"Next one goes in your knee." She told him. She made it a point to let him hear her jack another round.

Visibly weeping and whimpering Emilio raised his buttocks off the chair and slipped his underwear off. He dropped them to the floor beside the chair and looked up at her. His face was a picture of vile contempt. "You can't do this." He began. "They'll catch you and put you in a six by ten cell."

"Wrong, wrong and wrong again." She replied and as close as she was, she wasn't going to miss. The gun went off and put a round into his right knee. This time the force knocked him straight back and both Emilio and the chair toppled backwards. She watched him crumple to the floor and continued."First place they're never gonna find you. Second place they're never gonna find you and third, they're never gonna find you." She was finding some kind of humor in this and chuckled at her repetitive joke. "Now back in the chair while you can still move." She demanded.

Emilio had had enough. He wasn't going to get up and was ready to die right there. He thought about how badly his life had gone since coming into the country twenty years ago. he'd been a young man with ambition and desire.

However no one had been willing to give a wetback who didn't speak good English the opportunities needed for him to advance. After a while he'd resigned himself to being his own boss and started his landscaping company. It had worked well for ten years or so until he took on this woman as a client.

He'd been living alone and the women he met wanted nothing to do with a Lawnmower man. He was a man after all and had needs and desires but the women on the street wanted to be paid and he could barely afford rent, food and gas for his truck. Let alone upkeep on his mowing equipment. So that weak moment with this woman had turned his life upside down. It was obvious the way things were now that this was very probably going to be the end of it here and now.

TWENTY TWO

Ryan came to a halt at the sound of gunfire. It sounded close and off to his right. He made the adjustment in direction and jogged off. It had taken him a while and he'd been hoping the whole time his directional guesswork had been correct. Finding Albert dead on the floor of the cabin confirmed that he was definitely moving in the right direction and hot on her trail. Checking his phone map had taken a few minutes but after a ten minute jog he broke through the trees onto the dirt main street in Nighthawk.

He didn't doubt she had the ability to take care of herself, Albert's fallen, shot up body confirmed that. Ryan had never seen that side of her and wondered just how far she was willing to go. Was she a bonafide schitzo? He wasn't sure if he wanted to find out. His heart was falling for a woman who's personality he hadn't seen all of and he thought he knew.

He was about to call out to her but on second thought he didn't want to alert Santori of his whereabouts. He opted for moving on stealth until he was sure who and where everyone was. He at least had to determine who was firing at who.

He saw the same buildings Natasha had spotted when she came into town. The house with the crumpled roof was passed. The building with the wooden sidewalk was next as he moved slowly through the street. He was just about to enter it when a shot rang out from the building across the street. Whirling in that direction he dropped to a crouch and jerked out his service revolver.

*   *   *

She walked over to where Emilio was crumpled on the floor. She despised him for violating her. Her gut muscles were bound tighter than she could ever remember. Looking down on him she felt no empathy or sympathy for this creature. That wasn't her job. Her job was revenge. She didn't want to be the one handing out vigilante justice but somebody had to right the wrongs and she was willing to at least this time right the wrong that was done to her.

She stepped back to give him room to move. "Back in the chair!" She shouted. "I'm not done with you yet!"

"Fuck you!" He replied, pain, grief and misery slathered his words. "I give up." He scooted his back up against the wall so he could face her. His shoulder and knee were a bloody mess and he was in more than significant pain. He was done resisting, he was done running.

*   *   *

Gun drawn, Ryan approached the front door of the building. He could see the front door was gone and could hear Natasha's voice giving orders."Nat!" He hollered. "You in there?" There was no answer. He called again. "Natasha, it's me Steve Ryan. You o.k?"

"Ya." Came a quiet voice from the darkness. "I'm good but I think the bad guy is not so good."

"O.k." He replied. "I'm coming in." He kept his shooter's crouch and slipped through the front door.

Shining his duty light around the room he quickly spotted Natasha some ten feet inside. She was standing over a disheveled looking man who based on the amount of blood showing in his flashlight, was on the down side of life.

"Detective Ryan," she began, "meet Lawnmower Man. A.K.A. Emilio Santori convicted felon escapee from justice. Emilio meet Detective Ryan."

Emilio looked up at Ryan with glassy eyes and a wry smile. "You gotta do something man." He began. "This woman is crazy."

"Bang!" Another loud shot rang out making Ryan jump and Emilio cry out. The shot had gone into the wall a foot or so from the twice shot man.

"No derogatory remarks!" She barked at him. "You're not in a position to say anything that might piss me off more than I already am."

Ryan walked up next to her. "Ya think maybe he's had enough?" He asked quietly. He knew she was under a lot of stress and figured kid gloves were the best way to deal with her.

"Not if he's still breathing." She replied with contempt. "You saw what I looked like when you found me. You saw his body fluids stuck to my skin. All the result of this piece of shit. So no as long as he's breathing he hasn't had enough.

"So what? You're gonna torture him to death?" Ryan began. "You can't do that. It's just not right." He added.

"Well son of a gun. If we're going o judge our actions on what is right, then he's overdue." She countered. "By a long shot."

"C'mon Nat," Ryan started. "I know you're not that person and you know it. Lets head back to my unit and I'll call it in. I'll stand up for you and there won't be any charges because it was all self defense. I'll testify to it and my words as good as we need to get you through this."

"Oh really?" She said turning to face him. "Do you know for sure I'm not that kind of person. What makes you so sure?"

There was a sudden rustling sound from where Emilio had been propped up against the wall. He'd got himself up on his good leg and was about to make a lunge for Natasha. She saw the darkness of his body coming at her and quickly fired three rounds into the hulking figure coming at her.

Emilio stopped mid-lunge and dropped to the floor a foot in front of where she stood. Ryan was startled and taken back by the sound of Natasha's gun going off so close to him. It took a minute for them both to get control of their emotions.

"Outside." He barked and taking her by the elbow he ushered her towards and out through the front door. He was pissed and about to unload on her. "We both know he was a piece of shit but that didn't give you the right to take the law into your own hands! There's a justice system that I'm supposed to represent. You and your actions have compromised me. By the time we got back to my unit he would've probably bled out from the rounds you already put in him. That means you killing him was overkill and completely unnecessary." Steve was fuming. "How am I supposed to deal with this?" He asked.

She had stood there taking his berating without so much as raising an eyebrow. She waited until she was sure he was done and looked him in the eye. "Arrest me." She said flatly. "Take my gun, take me back to the city and lock me up. You'd have every right based on the two bodies I've added up."

He wanted to clock her for the smug arrogance she threw in his face. Knock her on her ass and adjust her attitude. Instead he turned away from her, took a couple of steps and blew a rush of air out his mouth.

He thought about the possibilities. Of where their relationship was and where it might be going. He loved her spunk, her style and the fact that he didn't have to walk her through life. She was pretty much a complete, together woman with a head on her shoulders and there wasn't an abundance of those around.

He envisioned a relationship, no a partnership where they would and could co-exist as two adults that might be able to satisfy each other's needs. She had enough fire to keep him in line and he could provide the stability that she obviously needed. He'd have to take a chance and hope he'd made the right choice.

He turned back to where she was standing on the dirt street in this abandon ghost town. She looked up at his face and saw the hard lines. "Let's go." He stated evenly and started for the tree line. "We can be back at the undercover by daylight and start the cleanup of this mess."

Natasha was tired. Tired of a lot of things. Tired of the long walk through the forest that she hadn't yet started. Tired of . . . . .

END

Stay tuned for the next narration of justice by the Lipstick Vigilante.

Made in United States
Troutdale, OR
03/17/2025